LITTLE GREEN MEN

Peter Cawdron
thinkingscifi.wordpress.com

Copyright © Peter Cawdron 2013

All rights reserved

The right of Peter Cawdron to be identified as the author of this work has been asserted by him in accordance with the Copyright, Designs and Patents Act 1988

First published as an eBook by Peter Cawdron using Smashwords

eBook ISBN: 978-1301766727
Physical ISBN-13: 978-1492844440

CreateSpace ISBN-10: 1492844446

US Edition

All the characters in this book are fictitious, and any resemblance to actual persons living or dead is purely coincidental

A TRIBUTE TO PHILIP K DICK

LIFE

Darkness surrounds two lonely astronauts. Sleet rains down on them, highlighted only by the spotlights mounted on the sides of their helmets. Johnson hangs back, while Michaels wades into the mist rising from a vast thermal pool.

Michaels is fascinated by the colors illuminated by his lights. Stratified layers of ochre, lime, and a mustard-like yellow line the pool, much like the holographs he's seen of Yellowstone on Earth. From orbit, radar imaging revealed a frozen plain covered in vents and geysers, with warm pools dotting the landscape, marked by a dark green border barely visible in the night.

"Come on in, the water's balmy," Michaels says, his voice breaking up over the radio.

"You are out of your *goddamn* mind," Johnson replies. "You heard what Vegas said, this whole geothermal area is unstable. You could fall into a vent."

"Actually, you're in more danger than me," Michaels replies, turning back toward Johnson in the waist-deep water, with his gloved hands skimming the surface. "If the crust can support water, it can support me. Where you're standing, however, hot vents have melted the ice. The crust could be wafer-thin and you wouldn't know it."

Johnson stands still. Michaels watches him surveying the cracks in the rock and ice beneath his feet, and laughs.

"I heard that. You're not funny, you know."

Michaels finds Johnson's response even funnier, but he gets back to work, looking for interesting formations to sample. He steps forward, stirring up silt. Michaels is methodical, watching his footing as he wades around the edge of the pool, not venturing any deeper than his waist. Although he's a scientist, his interest in the pools is more than professional curiosity. The variety of colors beneath the clear water are beautiful to behold. The child in him has to touch them, even if only through thick gloved hands and insulated boots. Graduated layers in the rock formations around him glisten like a rainbow. Michaels avoids muddy sections, not wanting to stir up sediment and mar the pristine edges, but he has to get samples. Samples justify his playful romp in the warm water. Besides, with the intense gravity of the planet, being suspended in fluid is physically relieving, and somewhat refreshing.

Lightning strikes one of the nearby pools, illuminating the darkness briefly with a pulsing blue flash. Michaels feels distinctly uncomfortable being so close to the strike, but he knows his suit will insulate him. The danger is that a strike could short out his hydraulics, or fry his electrical system.

"Damn, that was close," Johnson says.

An eerie glow radiates from the pool. Michaels could swear he can feel the electrical charge inside his suit, but he dismisses that as impossible. Up to a point, his suit will act as a Faraday cage, keeping electrical charges at bay.

The radio in his helmet crackles with an incoming message from the mining shuttle over a hundred kilometers away, but Michaels can't make out the words.

"Did you catch that?" he asks.

"They've broken through the mantle," Johnson says over the sound of the frozen methane pelting his helmet. "Vegas wants everyone back."

"Well, she'll have to wait. I'm collecting samples for analysis."

"Mickey," Johnson calls, using a diminutive form of Michaels' surname to deliberately piss him off, "You need to get your sorry ass out of that cesspool and back to the *Dei Gratia*."

"You have no idea what we're dealing with here, do you?" Michaels snaps. His gloved hands manipulate a portable mass spectrometer, scanning crystalline spikes breaking through the surface of the water. "These vents and thermal pools are astonishing. Most of this planet is an icy wasteland at 320 degrees below zero, but everywhere we find these vents, we find a warm chemical oasis at upwards of a balmy 90 degrees. And they're linked, networked through underground springs permeating the lithosphere. There's an absurd amount of volcanic energy driving this network.

"See that mist, that's the methane sublimating. I've found dissolved sulphur dioxides, lithium, carbon molecules laden with triphosphates, sodium salts, lots of fascinating chemistry. I'm picking up hydroxides and peroxides. This is a primordial soup. And these crystalline structures along the shoreline, they're like nothing I've ever seen before."

As Johnson steps forward, his spotlight passes over the shore, leaving it glowing in a soft green.

"What is that?" Johnson asks. "Is it like a plant or something? Photosynthesis?"

"Ah," Michaels replies. "You're thinking along the right lines, but it's not algae, that's radium glowing in the dark. Whatever this is, it's using chemosynthesis, or perhaps radio-synthesis. And it gets even more interesting, calcium and radium are chemically interchangeable, but with devastating consequences for life, as radium is radioactive. Here, though, the radium is banished to the edges by some unknown mechanism, allowing calcium carbonate to form freely in the depths. Isn't that remarkable?"

"Wonderful, beautiful," Johnson says, sarcasm dripping from his words. "Now if you're finished playing in the mud, the adults would like to get back to work."

"You ignorant Neanderthal," Michaels mutters under his breath, continuing to scan the waist-deep waters.

"I heard that."

"Good. You were supposed to."

Michaels wades into the shallows on the far side of the pool. Warm water laps at his legs, just below his knees. Even with the heat bloom coming off the water, ice forms on his suit and his exoskeleton kicks up a gear. The lights from his helmet expose a fluorescent-blue crust running along the rim of the bank, highlighting a layer beneath the green, glowing radium deposits.

Plumes of steam rise from the mouth of the main vent fifty feet away. Michaels pulls out a pickaxe and takes samples, scraping the coating into carefully marked specimen bags.

"We've got to go," Johnson pleads.

"Five more minutes."

"That's what you said an hour ago," Johnson replies. "Quit screwing around in that decrepit spa pool. We're not down here for playtime. There's real work to be done back at the shuttle."

Michaels ignores him, adjusting his gravity compensator. He tweaks the mechanical skeleton surrounding his suit, relieving his aching legs. Coming out of the water, he's lost buoyancy and the 1.4G field reminds him this planet is hostile in numerous ways. His heart pumps harder, even when resting. Breathing is a chore.

"Michaels, you need to follow orders."

"I'm going to need your help here," Michaels says, again ignoring Johnson. "I want to take a sample from some of these large outcrops above the waterline. Power up your mining laser."

"I ain't going in there," Johnson replies. "I've seen this movie. I know what happens. Some slippery green alien critter's going to pop out at the last minute and shove its goddamn phallic symbol down my throat!"

"Don't be stupid. I need your help here," Michaels repeats,

turning back toward him.

"You need my help, all right," Johnson moans as he begins wading over toward Michaels. "You need help tying your goddamn shoelaces."

Michaels snaps. "You... You arrogant, obnoxious, stubborn, prideful mule! This isn't a lark. This isn't some stupid game, or one of your bravado bonding/bitching sessions with the miners. This is potentially the most important discovery in the history of mankind."

"What?" Johnson yells back at him as the water swirls around his waist, "This shit hole?"

"This *shit hole*, as you so eloquently put it, is the genesis of life. If my suspicions are correct, we're dealing with the alien equivalent of *hydrogenothermaceae*."

Johnson turns his head from side to side as he approached Michaels, he looks nervous. He's scanning the pool for any sign of movement.

"Nothing's going to jump out at you."

"How do you know that?" Johnson demands. "One minute, you're telling me I'm stupid, the next you're telling me you've found aliens. How do you know something isn't going to jump out of the shadows? There could be a goddamn face hugger down there and you wouldn't know. Damn it, this shit always ends badly in Hollywood."

Johnson breathes heavily as he wades into the shallower water, but that doesn't stop him from talking. Michaels assumes he finds refuge in running his mouth.

"The Confederacy has searched over two hundred star systems, almost three thousand surveyed planets, and God knows how many moons, and there hasn't been a shred of evidence for extraterrestrial life, but you think this muddy hellhole is different? Where are your little green men? I don't see ET bathing in this cesspool."

Michaels doesn't want to get drawn into a lengthy debate. When Vegas assigned Johnson to buddy with him, he knew it was a mistake, but Vegas insisted. At the very least, her decision has given Michaels the chance to explore for something other than volatiles. Interplanetary regulations dictate crew diversity, something about avoiding *group-think*, but Michaels finds the crew grating. He would rather be assigned to a research mission than an exploration vessel. He tries to explain himself to Johnson.

"Life has existed on Earth for almost four billion years. For more than three billion years, life looked pretty much like this, just a pile of sludge slowly forming various fundamental structures—the simplest forms of life. I can't be sure until I get these samples back to the *Dei Gratia*, but the chemical markers here are similar to DNA. There's amino acids, simple nucleic sugars, complex carbon strings. There's every chance these pools are populated with the alien equivalent of archaean microbes, not even something as complex as bacteria—something far simpler."

"Great, we've found a bunch of bugs," Johnson grunts, coming up beside him.

"Yes, precisely."

"So you're telling me that the first *goddamn* aliens mankind encounters are germs?"

"Well, statistically speaking," Michaels begins, naively assuming Johnson's actually interested in his discovery, "it's not that surprising. The sheer weight of time required to produce intelligent life would suggest we're far more likely to encounter '*bugs*,' as you so eloquently put it, rather than your fabled *little green men*. The chance of mankind co-hosting the galaxy with another sentient race is ludicrously small. There's much more–"

"Can we get on with this?" Johnson growls. "I'm hungry."

Michaels is angry, but he calms himself. He has to learn to stop letting greasers like Johnson get to him. He uses his wrist controls to turn on the recorder on the side of his helmet and says, "OK, this is it. One last sample."

Michaels steps up onto a thin ledge between the thermal pools, carefully finding his footing on the fragile crust. Johnson steps up beside him without any concern for the ground crunching beneath his boots. Already, the extremely cold wind has caused the liquid on their suits to freeze. Their actuators, though, compensated for the added resistance, so they hardly noticed as thin sheets of ice fell from their suits.

"The structure in front of me," Michaels begins, "is approximately twelve feet in diameter, standing eight feet tall. It has the consistency of coral, branching out from a broad base just above the waterline. Specialist Johnson is going to use a standard 3800 nanometer deuterium-fluoride mining laser to remove a section roughly the size of my arm."

"Who the hell are you talking to?" Johnson asks, tapping Michaels on the helmet as if he's knocking on a door to see if anyone's home.

Michaels is flustered, embarrassed. "Posterity," he splutters. "I'm recording this event for future generations. This is momentous. This is Nobel Prize material. I must record this. Future generations will want to review this footage. They'll want to know precisely how this moment unfolded."

"Why?"

"To understand," Michaels continues. "This event will be studied like Columbus discovering the Americas, like the Pilgrims landing at Plymouth Rock. It will be analyzed like Armstrong setting foot on the Moon, or Chiang on Mars."

"Who's swollen with pride now?" Johnson asks as he powers up his mining laser.

"Just cut here," Michaels says bluntly.

Michaels holds the coral arm as Johnson slices through it with the laser. A red dot projects from the sighting mechanism, highlighting where the invisible laser beam will strike the structure. Within seconds, the laser has seared through the coral.

Michaels turns to Johnson, holding the arm up in triumph. He's speechless. A smile stretches across his face as he holds his trophy with pride.

"Are you happy now?" Johnson asks. "Can we get back to the shuttle?"

"Yes, yes. Let's get back to the *Dei Gratia*."

Johnson turns and steps back into the pond. Michaels wades in behind him, keeping the lump of coral out of the water. Mud stirs up from the bottom, swirling around their legs.

The wind blows wave upon wave of frozen sleet down on them, reducing visibility to a few feet. Eddies dance in the air. Flakes of methane snow light up in the glare of their headlights before melting in the heat radiating from the pool.

As they reach the far shore and move out of the thermal bloom surrounding the vent, the temperature drops rapidly. Michaels increases the pulse rate on his de-icing circuits, Johnson merely powers up his gravity-assister to increase his suit's dexterity. Crystals form on their visors. Michaels brushes his gloved hand across the visor, noting that within ten feet of the outlying pool the ambient temperature has dropped almost two hundred degrees. The warmth that had previously radiated through the soles of his boots is replaced with a chill as the environmental controls in his suit kick into overdrive.

A tiny scout craft sits on the frozen plateau in the distance—a small atmospheric craft designed to conduct surveys beyond the sensor range of the main shuttle.

The crunch of loose shale underfoot soon gives way to coarse ice. Methane continues to fall in the form of sleet. Lightning ripples overhead.

"Did you see that?" Michaels asks, breathing heavily with the coral arm resting over his shoulder. He wants to stop and adjust his gravity-assister, but he doesn't want to fall behind Johnson. There's movement on the edge of his vision.

"I can't see a *goddamn* thing," Johnson replies, using his wrist computer to detect the homing beacon on the scout. "We're two hundred meters out. The sooner we get out of here, the better. This place gives me the creeps."

Michaels turns from the waist, moving his shoulders and allowing the spotlights on his helmet to pan around. Through the driving snow, shadows flicker in the darkness. He fights against the headwind to come alongside Johnson. The earpiece in his helmet crackles as a transmission comes through from the *Dei Gratia*.

"Michaels? Johnson? Where are you guys?" Vegas asks. Her voice is that of a Southern Belle, calm and soothing.

"Making our way back to the scout, ma'am," Johnson replies.

"We're pumping tritium," Vegas says from somewhere in the warm confines of the bridge on the *Dei Gratia*. "When you come back, come in slow and cold. I don't want any flare-ups."

Johnson screams suddenly and violently.

At first, Michaels assumes it's feedback, or some kind of short circuit in his radio, but the pitch and intensity of Johnson's scream overwhelms the choppy, broken transmission from the *Dei Gratia*.

Michaels drops the coral on the ice. Instinctively, he raises his hands as he tries to block his ears, but his gloves hit the smooth outer shell of his helmet. His spotlight catches flashes of brilliant red blood streaked across the blue-white ice.

Over the screaming, Michaels can hear Vegas calling out, "Cut his transmission! Cut his *goddamn* transmission." She's yelling at someone on board the *Dei Gratia*.

Johnson rolls on the ice. Blood stains his white suit. Shards of crimson ice crystals are smeared across the outside of his visor.

Michaels is stunned. He's in shock. It takes a few seconds before he realizes Johnson's right arm is gone, severed off just below the shoulder.

The screaming ceases abruptly, and Michaels can hear himself hyperventilating inside his suit. He drops to his knees beside Johnson. With gloved hands, he tries to help, but what can he do? His hands are clumsy and uncoordinated. He wipes away the fine, frozen blood from Johnson's visor.

Johnson's still screaming, but there's no sound. Johnson's eyes are pressed shut, his mouth is open, but there's no noise, just the sound of the wind howling across the desolate plain. Someone onboard the *Dei Gratia* has cut Johnson's audio feed.

"What the *hell* is going on?" Vegas demands over the radio waves.

Something brushes against Michaels. He turns and catches sight of someone disappearing into the darkness. He swings around, staggering to his feet. There are more of them, crowding around him, buffeting him as they race past, but the light from his helmet seems to repel them.

"Michaels. Sit-rep."

Michaels fumbles with a flare from his leg pocket. His thick gloves struggle with the twist-top. Suddenly, the frozen darkness is illuminated with the brilliance of a magnesium alloy burning at over a thousand degrees.

"Michaels!" Vegas commands.

Michaels holds the flare aloft, pushing back the darkness by thirty feet around them. Bloodstains cover the blue-white ice. Brilliant arcs of red and crimson have sprayed out across the frozen ground.

Johnson convulses.

Michaels sticks the flare into the ice and kneels beside him.

The flare is both a blessing and a curse, blinding him to anything beyond its reach, casting dark shadows across the ice. The falling methane takes on blood red hues in the light of the flare, terrifying him.

"Michaels. Are you there?"

"Yeah."

His voice is shaking. Adrenaline surges through his veins. His hands tremble. Johnson lies beside him. He's either unconscious or dead, Michaels doesn't want to hazard a guess as to which.

"Stream your video," is the call over the airways. The voice is soft, feminine, soothing. It's Dr. Jane Summers. "Can you hear me, Michaels? I want you to stream your video."

Michaels mumbles to himself as his thick gloved fingers punch at his wrist-pad controls. He's trembling.

"That's it. We can see your feed. What happened to Johnson?"

Michaels is numb. He can't speak. He simply bends forward, directing the camera on his helmet down at the still body before him. On the bridge of the *Dei Gratia,* several people talk in the background, including Vegas and Dr. Summers. They hurriedly discuss the video, trying to make sense of what has happened. After a few seconds, Summers comes back on the microphone.

"OK, Michaels, I want you to get closer. I need to get a good look at Johnson's shoulder. Do you understand? I need to see the injury."

Michaels doesn't respond. He reaches out and rocks Johnson on his side so the frozen, bloodied stump below the wounded astronaut's shoulder is clearly visible. Michaels holds him there, shaking. Again, there's a heated discussion away from the microphone.

"Mike," Summers begins. His abbreviated surname doesn't seem so relevant any more. "Listen to me. Whatever happened out there, Johnson's suit is still transmitting vitals. He's alive. Do you understand me? He's not dead. He is still alive. The wound has fused to the fabric. The extreme cold has sealed the rupture, cauterizing the arteries and stopping the bleeding. His suit has automatically vented the noxious gases and restored partial internal pressure. I need you to get him back to the *Dei Gratia*. Do you understand me? You need to get him back to your scout craft, and then back here to us on the *Dei Gratia*."

Vegas is talking away from the microphone. He can hear her in the background saying, "What the hell happened out there? I want to know what caused this."

Michaels can't speak. He simply drags Johnson up beside him, pulling Johnson's one good arm over his shoulder. Michaels stumbles on through the blizzard toward the scout, using his gravity assisters to compensate for Johnson's weight, leaving the flare stuck in the ice.

As the darkness closes in so do the creatures. They buffet and bump him, coming from behind and brushing up against him as they dart by, forever staying out of the light of his helmet.

Michaels presses on, terrified. As he approaches the scout, the landing lights come on automatically and the creatures scurry for the shadows. Over his headset, he can hear Vegas and Summers talking about what they're seeing on his video feed, but their words are indistinct, a muddle of sound.

Michaels doesn't worry about decontamination or de-suiting. Once he's closed the hatch and cycled the air, he removes his gloves and opens the faceplate on both helmets.

"That's it. You're doing great," Summers says, watching from afar. "I need you to get Johnson on life support."

Johnson looks like a corpse. The color has washed from his face. His skin is clammy and feels like plastic, but Summers is still receiving remote biofeedback from his suit, and that's good enough for Michaels. If Summers says Johnson's alive, Michaels believes her. In his almost catatonic state, he has to believe something.

"Put your helmet opposite Johnson so I can continue to see him."

Instructions are good. They give Michaels something to rally his mind around, something to focus on to shut out the anguish he feels welling up. Michaels dutifully complies. He then struggles through the smaller door on the inner lock, and grabs a headset so he can continue talking to Summers and Vegas as he moves around the scout craft.

"Listen, Mike," Summers says. "Harris is going to remote pilot you back from here. I want you to set up a medi-cast monitor beside Johnson. Add four liters of plasma to the resource tray. I'll be able to remotely control the unit from here."

Michaels obeys dutifully, grabbing the monitor from the under-floor locker. There's already a four-liter plasma bag in place. Summers is being overly prescriptive with Johnson's life hanging in the balance, but Michaels doesn't mind. He can't blame her for treating him as though he's a child. He needs it. His hands are still shaking. In his current state, he wouldn't trust himself to count to three without some kind of independent verification.

Michaels barely feels the craft lift off the ice as he staggers back into the airlock, still wearing his suit, minus only his helmet and gloves. The floor tilts slightly, and he knows they're on their way back to the *Dei Gratia*.

"Time is of the essence," a disembodied voice says in his ear—Vegas.

Michaels has to mount the medi-cast. He grabs a pair of shears and cuts through the thick suit material around Johnson's good arm, exposing his thermal undergarment. A small nick in the undergarment allows him to tear through to the skin. Sweat drips from his brow as he clamps the medi-cast in place. Immediately, the soft whine of machinery begins and a series of probes pierce the skin while a pump starts administering meds and fluids.

"Good, good. Now I need you to apply a tourniquet to his other shoulder."

Michaels wipes his forehead with the back of his wrist. He looks around, wondering what he can use to tie off the stump that was once Johnson's arm. Based on the befuddled look on his face, Dr. Summers must read his mind, as she adds, "You'll find a section of soft rubber hose in the suit repair kit. Just make sure the tourniquet is pulled tight or he'll bleed out once his wound thaws."

Michaels mumbles. He continues working with the shears, cutting away the suit across the top of Johnson's chest and around the bloody stump of his arm. Johnson's arm was amputated above the bicep, cutting through the shoulder muscle at an angle. Already, the wound is weeping. Blood trickles to the floor. The flesh looks black, as though it has been charred in a fire. The smell gets to Michaels, forcing him to turn away from time to time so as to avoid vomiting.

"You're doing great." Summers' voice is soothing in the midst of the turmoil. The craft rocks from turbulence, reminding him they're in flight.

Michaels rolls Johnson on his side, placing him in the recovery position, moving the medi-cast, and rocking Johnson's good arm behind and beneath him. After cutting away the remainder of the space suit, Michaels straps the rubber tubing around the upper shoulder, pulling it as tight as he can and tying it off in a knot.

"That's good. You're doing really well."

Michaels doesn't care. He slumps back against the far side of the airlock, feeling the vibration of the engines through the hull, along with the winds buffeting the scout. Blood stains his hands.

The fifteen-minute flight time seems to pass in seconds, which confuses Michaels. He feels as though he's only just set up the monitor and tourniquet when Vegas and Summers come rushing through the airlock to take over for him. For a moment, he wonders where they came from. He doesn't realize he's already back in the landing bay of the *Dei Gratia*.

Two other crewmen enter with Vegas and Summers, but Michaels is so dazed he barely notices them. If they say anything to him, it doesn't register. They carry Johnson away on a stretcher, leaving Michaels leaning against the curved wall of the airlock, his blood-red hands resting in his lap. Eventually, Summers returns. She takes him to the sick bay and gives him a shot of Valium to put him to sleep.

DEATH

Michaels wakes feeling refreshed. For a moment, he doesn't remember anything unusual. The incident at the thermal pool has faded like a bad dream, but when Dr. Summers walks in, and Michaels realizes he's lying on a bed in the medical bay, reality comes flooding back.

"How is Johnson?"

"How are you?" Summers asks, gently touching his forehead. She has her hair down, which is unusual for her. She normally keeps her long blonde locks pulled back in a ponytail. Dr. Summers is all business, always professional, but she looks rattled, scared. Her eyes are bloodshot. She seems preoccupied, distracted. She looks down at her electronic clipboard. Although she seems concerned about him, Michaels gets the impression she's going through the motions. She asks, "Are you feeling OK?" But she's the one with a tremor in her voice.

"I'm fine. How's Johnson?" That Summers is evasive worries Michaels. He fears the worst. He and Johnson may not have been friends, but they've been crewmates for almost seven years, which makes any aggravation between them akin to sibling animosity, and par for the course. Deep down, Michaels feels a tinge of responsibility for Johnson's horrific injury. He should have left the thermal pools when Vegas recalled them. If they'd departed sooner, they might have avoided the attack.

"If you're up to it, Vegas would like you to come up to the bridge."

"And Johnson?" Michaels repeats a third time.

"Johnson…"

Summers thinks about her choice of words. It seems to take a deliberate effort for her to recall the details. "Johnson's in a chemically-induced coma. He lost two-thirds of his blood out there on the ice. At this stage, we're not sure if there was irreparable brain damage. His ECG scan is not good. The area that was cauterized by the cold suffered irreversible cellular damage and had to be cut back to the base of his neck. I've stabilized him but the physiological shock to his body was massive. I simply don't know if he'll survive, or what mental state he'll be in when he wakes. I'm sorry."

Michaels is silent. He sits up on the edge of the bed, but his head hangs low. A soft rhythmic ping from the other side of the curtain tells him Johnson is just beyond the thin, flimsy plastic. Part of him wants to see Johnson, if for no other reason that to show him some solidarity, but guilt eats away at Michaels' heart.

"I'm sorry," Summers offers a second time, her soft hand resting on his shoulder. She shouldn't be. It wasn't her fault. She's done all she can.

Michaels stands up slowly. His body aches. Although the

medical quarters are warm, he feels cold.

"You're still in shock," Summers warns him. "Physically, you're fine. But your eyes are partially dilated. Mentally, you're still coming to grips with what happened out there on the ice."

"What did happen?" Michaels asks.

"That's what we all want to know. Vegas is waiting."

They walk to the bridge. Without the gravity modifiers built into his EVA suit, Michaels struggles. The intense surface gravity makes each step laborious. It's as though he's carrying almost half again his weight—an invisible backpack full of stones pressed down on his shoulders. In his weakened state, each step is an accomplishment. He shuffles his feet as though he's dragging around cast iron shackles. Normally, the increased gravity doesn't seem so bad, but Michaels feels drained.

Summers walks beside him. She looks numb, as though she's drugged and simply going through the motions. Something's wrong, something other than what happened to Johnson.

"What's the matter?" he asks.

"I don't know," she replies. "I'm scared—worried about what else we'll find out there. There have been other sightings. The sooner we get off this rock the better."

Michaels starts to speak, wanting her to elaborate, but there's something in the tone of her voice, in the weary look on her face that says it's all too much. Even her choice of words is telling. Summers speaks of sightings as though someone else has seen these creatures, but her fragile demeanor suggests she's seen them herself. If he hadn't been out there on the ice with Johnson, he'd insist on details, but he can relate to how overwhelmed she must feel. For all his scientific curiosity, Michaels understands the emotional, human side of facing fear. There are no simple answers.

"Yeah," he says, lost in his own recollections of the alien swarm, trying to reconcile the living nightmare that engulfed him on the ice.

The interior of the *Dei Gratia* looks normal, and that reassures Michaels. Pristine white panels hide the cabling and ventilation ducts running behind the walls and above the ceiling. Junction boxes and access panels are set at regular intervals. The lighting includes a small amount of UV to stimulate the production of Vitamin D, and that gives the light a bluish tone that has always felt unnatural, but now it's strangely comforting. Technically, the light is a cool blue, and it makes the inside of the ship appear sterile. It isn't, of course—nothing humanity has ever touched has remained sterile. Humans have dragged viruses, bacteria, mites, protozoa, and archea everywhere. Tiny microbes are exploring the galaxy alongside *Homo sapiens*, which is what led to the sterilization procedures in the airlocks. Michaels understands better than most that sterilization works both ways, keeping microbes out of planetary environments, and keeping the noxious fumes, carcinogens and toxic chemicals out of the habitat. In the back of his mind, Michaels is vaguely aware he ignored that protocol in the scout and is haunted by the prospect he may have contaminated the ship with an unknown pathogen.

Vegas is seated in front of the navigation desk. She looks like she's aged ten years. The natural silver-grey highlights in her hair look as though they've turned white. Like Dr. Summers, her eyes speak of horror. Vegas is normally militaristic in her leadership, now she looks shaken.

"How are you feeling?" she asks.

"Like shit."

"Aren't we all," Vegas replies, sipping some coffee.

"How long was I out?"

"Four hours," Summers says, sitting next to Vegas, "You slept like a baby."

Vegas adds, "The storm's been playing havoc with communications. There's still one survey team out there on the ice."

Michaels sits at one of the seats surrounding the navigation desk. The three-dimensional hologram before him depicts the terrain out to five hundred kilometers. The sections explored by the aerial survey teams appear in fine detail, but their paths are erratic, following various mineral deposits rather than systematically sweeping the terrain. It is as though Picasso or Jackson Pollock has taken to the map in a flurry of insanity, daubing splashes of paint across a rough sketch.

Vegas hands Michaels a cup of black coffee. The rich, dark fluid sloshes in the heavy gravity.

"This whole goddamn mission is turning into a clusterfuck," she says. "The containment tank ruptured. We were venting H3 for almost an hour before we managed to seal the leak. If we fired up the drive in this state there's a good chance she'd go nova, so for now, we're not going anywhere."

"What about the *Argo*?" Michaels asks, referring to the interstellar mothership circling the planet.

Vegas scratches the back of her head, saying, "I've spoken with Phillips. The remaining scouts could make the run into low-orbit, but the *Argo* needs fuel. We can't panic. We need to sit tight, vent the hold, compress that H3, and then we can leave with a full load."

Michaels is silent. As science officer, he knows the dangers of a leak near the fusion core. As Vegas finishes speaking, the communication relay flickers into life. The coms officer turns to her, saying, "It's Jacobs."

"Well, it's about bloody time," she replies. "Put him on speaker."

"Hey, commander," a distant voice says. "You are not going to believe what I've found."

"What the hell happened to your lost-coms procedure?" Vegas replies, ignoring him. "You should have been back hours ago."

"Sorry, commander," comes a reply which sounds more fawning than apologetic.

"Like hell you are. Get your ass back here. I don't need anyone else running around in this goddamn storm."

She's lying, or at least not telling him all she knows. Michaels wants to press her about it, to convince her she should be open with Jacobs, tell him what happened to Johnson, but he doesn't want to spook the others, either on the bridge or out on the planet. He raises his hand slightly from the nav-desk, catching her attention with his fingers. Vegas sees him, but she ignores his gesture to mute the transmission and discuss emergency protocols.

Summers bites at her nails. She glances at Michaels, shaking her head softly in disagreement with Vegas. Her eyes are haunted. It's as though she hasn't slept in days.

"You're going to want to see this," Jacobs says, streaming his video.

The intensity of the storm causes the images from his helmet camera to freeze erratically, pixelating and forming chunky outlines. From what Michaels can see in the grainy image, Jacobs is setting up a repeater station, a booster mounted on a tripod to raise the signal-to-noise ratio and improve the video quality. He's probably using line-of-sight transmission back to his scout craft, and from there relaying to the *Dei Gratia* via over-the-horizon VHF.

The main screen flickers as Jacobs says, "I may have found all the tritium you need."

"What the hell are you doing out there alone?" Vegas asks, ignoring his comment.

"Oh," Jacobs replies, pausing for a moment. His voice sounds distant, as though he's lost in thought. "Hubbard's here. Hang on, I'll show you the big picture."

The image switches to a wide-angle remote shot from the scout craft roughly a hundred meters away. Through the choppy, disjointed flicker, Michaels can see a lone astronaut standing in front of an airlock on the side of a derelict space freighter. Jacobs waves his gloved hand for the camera. The view has to be coming from the forward-facing array on the scout.

Vegas gasps.

Sheets of ice cling to the metal skin of the derelict starship. Dark shadows obscure the sealed airlock. Jacobs stands on a raised gantry in front of the airlock. Michaels is confused, wondering, where the hell is Hubbard?

A second astronaut steps into view, stepping out of the shadows and waving a gloved hand in a seemingly identical motion to Jacobs. Michaels blinks, unsure of of what he's seeing. Hubbard seemed to appear from nowhere. The contrast in the image is awful, making it difficult to distinguish shapes. Hubbard must have been standing in the shadows. He continues waving, but he doesn't say anything.

Jacobs taps at his wrist computer and the spotlights on the scout illuminate the frozen hull of the freighter.

The storm has eased for Jacobs and Hubbard, giving Michaels a physical indicator as to how distant they are—they must be several hundred kilometers away. Flashes of lightning ripple through a brooding cloudbank beyond the mysterious freighter. Flecks of methane snow drift through the spotlight beams.

The access gantry sits on a telescopic frame that scissors back and forth, with metal poles crisscrossing to provide stability. Michaels can see the frame swaying in the wind. With the ice some fifty feet below, the gantry must be anchored by bolts reaching through the ice into the bedrock. They've been there awhile. They should have called this in immediately.

Dawn is breaking, casting long shadows down the length of the space freighter. Methane ice has buried the landing gear of the craft.

Icicles hang from the bulkhead. None of the viewport hatches are open and the cargo hold hasn't been lowered. Apart from the ice, the starship looks like it's just landed.

"Pretty cool, huh?" Hubbard says, his voice crackling with the low signal-to-noise ratio.

Harris brings up the view from Hubbard's helmet camera on another monitor.

"What the hell?" Vegas mutters. She catches herself, and her professionalism comes to the forefront as she asks, "Have you identified the ship?"

"No," came the scratchy reply from Jacobs.

"Harris, run a search for any long-haul freighters that have gone missing within a parsec."

"On it."

Immediately, the bridge on the *Dei Gratia* comes alive with a sense of urgency.

"Should we call this in?" Dr. Summers asks. Michaels is thinking the same thing. They should report this to the *Argo*.

Vegas replies swiftly, "Not until we have something concrete. The last thing we need is for conjecture to enter the decision-making process. Let's get some clarity first."

Summers is tight-lipped. She doesn't agree. Vegas is strong willed. Michaels liked Vegas from the first day he met her, but he finds her overbearing at times.

Vegas personally requested Michaels for her crew, having met him only in passing at a party out beyond the Oort Cloud. Her smile exudes confidence. If she'd been born a man, there's no doubt she would have commanded the *Argo* instead of being relegated to planetary command. Sexism is strangely persistent, and it's a two edged sword. Michaels can see Vegas has no intention of bringing Philips in on this discovery, and Michaels doubts she's said anything about Johnson to him. Oh, she'll probably feign forgetfulness in the heat of the moment, but there's no way she's going to have a man telling her what to do on her watch. Philips might have overall command, but Vegas is the commander on the spot.

Ordinarily, Michaels would have no problem trusting her judgment, but this time he isn't so sure. Michaels wonders whether Vegas is confident or proud, and he wonders whether her obstinate streak will get them all killed.

The slight sound of breathing comes in over the radio, and Michaels realizes Hubbard and Jacobs are still standing outside the airlock listening to the cockpit discussion. He wonders how much they can read between the lines. Clearly, they don't know about Johnson. He starts to say something but Vegas cuts him off, looking at him with an icy gaze as she speaks to the distant team. She's determined to maintain control.

"Are there any signs of damage to the lock? Can you see any signs of a struggle?"

Hubbard must pick up on something in her tone of voice as he replies, "You mean like a fight? Who the hell would they be fighting?"

"Something bad must have happened to them," Michaels blurts

out before Vegas can stop the transmission.

"Get out of there!" Dr. Summers cries.

Vegas holds up her hand, signaling for quiet.

"Is something wrong?" Hubbard asks.

Jacobs replies to Hubbard before Vegas can say anything.

"You're standing in front of an airlock on an abandoned star freighter, and you want to know if anything's wrong?"

"You know what I mean," Hubbard replies defensively.

Vegas takes hold of the low ceiling, her hands just inches from a series of overhead controls and dials. She speaks slowly and deliberately.

"You should know we've run into problems elsewhere... about a hundred clicks southwest of your location. Michaels and Johnson were attacked by an unknown species."

"Is this some kind of joke?" Hubbard asks, an echo coming through with his words.

"It's no joke," Vegas confirms. "We've been recalling scouts. You guys are the last ones to come home."

"Aliens," Jacobs snaps. "You're talking about *fucking aliens?*"

Dr. Summers points to a console next to the navigation desk. A series of dynamic graphs show the vital signs of the two remote astronauts, both have spikes in adrenaline, along with increases in blood pressure and heart rates.

Vegas nods, not that they can see her. She speaks in a calm

voice.

"We don't know what we're dealing with just yet, but yes, it appears we've encountered indigenous life forms. To them, we're the aliens. Johnson has been injured. We're pulling out once we've secured the tritium."

Jacobs' heart rate hits 138 beats per minute. Hubbard's heartbeat spikes briefly, but quickly drops back into the low 90s, which isn't unusual given the intense gravity.

"Don't you want to know?" Hubbard asks. "I mean, we've found a *fucking* starship abandoned on this planet. Don't you want to know what happened to it? How it got here?"

Dr. Summers shakes her head, as does Michaels. Vegas takes her cue from the doctor, saying, "Ah, the general consensus here is we return to orbit so we can transmit records back to the Hub."

"And what?" Hubbard asks. "Wait seven years for a reply? What *fucking* good is that going to do?"

Vegas mouths the word 'none' without making a sound. She agrees with Hubbard, but she's trying to do what's right for the crew.

"We're OK," Hubbard continues. "We're in good shape and capable of continuing our EVA. We need to go inside this craft and figure out what happened to them."

"Are you bloody mad?" Jacobs asks, and Michaels can see this is precisely what Vegas is trying to avoid.

"Listen," she says to the two distant astronauts. "Nobody's going in that ship until we figure out where it came from and how it ended up here."

"And how are you going to do that, commander?" Hubbard asks. "You're always going on about trusting the man on the ground. Well, I'm the man on the ground, and I say we go in. I say, we won't learn jack-shit about this from orbit."

Vegas clenches her fists, still leaning against the console above her head. The strain shows on her face—the conflict raging within—whether to inform Phillips on the *Argo*, whether to stick it out and continue mining, or pull back into orbit, whether to investigate the derelict star freighter, or abandon the find. Command is a lonely role, which is precisely why Michaels has avoided applying for a senior position, settling on that of scientific advisor. She's damned if she does, damned if she doesn't. Phillips will read her the riot act when he finds out what happened to Johnson, and yet that was one isolated incident. Granted it was a violent, bloody incident, but it was only one action occurring in a remote area, well away from the main shuttle. The best anyone knows, it's an isolated incident that doesn't pose a threat to the *Dei Gratia*.

Was it one incident? Dr. Summers said there had been other sightings, and Michaels wonders what she meant. Where? Who saw them? What did they see? Has there been any more violence? He wants to ask Vegas, but the pace of events is unfolding too quickly, and the moment is lost.

"Damn it, Hubbard," Vegas snaps. "Get your ass back here. That's an order."

Michaels has to admire Vegas. She's walking a fine line. It

would be easy to give in to Hubbard and just go with it, but she's doing what's right even though it seems to run against her own desires.

They watch the video screen as one of the astronauts holds onto the railing on the gantry and begins descending to the blue ice. The second astronaut fiddles with something on the side of the airlock, standing in the narrow portico by the outer doors. As there's silence on the radio. Michaels figures they've switched to local coms and have been conversing between themselves, cutting the *Dei Gratia* out of the loop. Vegas is pissed. She knows they've cut their outbound transmission.

"What the hell is going on?" she asks. "Jacobs, is that you on the gantry?"

"Yes, I'm descending on the gantry," is the calm reply.

"You can't do this," Vegas protests. "You can't abandon Hubbard!"

"If that fucker wants to get himself killed, that's his choice. You won't catch me in a haunted house. I'll send the gantry back for him."

Vegas is enraged. Her face is flushed as she calls out, "Jacobs, go back and get him. Hubbard, don't do this. Step inside that ship and I'll bust your ass back to squab."

Jacobs ignores Vegas, continuing his descent.

"Jacobs, get back up there!"

"Come on, Vegas," Hubbard replies. "You and I both know we can't walk away from this thing, we have to see inside, we have to know what happened."

Hubbard wrestles with an oversized emergency crank, trying to override the door of the lock. He's in a ridiculously stupid position. If he steps backwards more than a foot he'll fall. In heavy gravity, even a fall of ten feet can cause serious injuries. Jacobs is already twenty feet below him and descending fast, leaving him stranded.

Hubbard is alone on an icy shelf with wind gusts buffeting his suit. He grunts, straining to crack the frozen door seals. Slowly, the outer door opens.

Harris is busy at one of the consoles, searching the core database for any record of lost starships. Michaels reaches over and takes control of the main screen from Harris. He cycles through the other cameras on the scout craft, trying to get a better look at the abandoned freighter.

"How far do you think you'll get without power?" Vegas asks, watching the tiny figure on the screen as Michaels changes cameras. He scans the body of the vessel, looking for any form of identification.

"Think of the salvage rights," Hubbard says as a dark shadow appears between the two white panels marking the outer airlock doors. Hubbard is working hard, breathing heavily as he winds the crank inside the emergency access panel on the side of the lock.

"Think of a month's pay being docked for insubordination," Vegas replies.

Hubbard laughs.

Vegas signals with her hand, running her finger across her throat, and Harris mutes the line. They can still hear Hubbard breathing heavily and Jacobs swearing at him as he descends on the portable gantry, but the *Dei Gratia* is no longer transmitting.

"We've got to figure out what the hell is going on here," Vegas says.

Michaels nods in agreement. He zooms in on a section of the hull near the bridge, noting there's writing below the portholes, but he can't make out the letters beneath the ice. He begins shifting between frequencies, examining the craft in infrared and ultraviolet, as well as constructing composite images rendered in false-color as he seeks to identify the name hidden beneath the ice.

"*Céleste*," Dr. Summers cries, she jumps out of her seat and darts up to the screen, looking closely at the letters, touching the monitor as though she is clearing away the ice. "It's the *Céleste*."

"I can sharpen that image," Harris says.

Michaels gestures to the controls, allowing Harris to resume command. Harris changes filter settings and enhances the image. Summers is right, which surprises Michaels as he could barely make out any of the letters when she first identified the *Céleste*.

Harris turns back to his console and conducts a shipping search on *Céleste*.

"The *Céleste* is registered out of New France on Titan, commissioned for the northern sector… She was listed as missing almost two decades ago. She's a long way from home. Says here she's a frigate."

"She's a C-Class," Jacobs says, listening in on the conversation from the icy plain beside the abandoned starship. "I served my apprenticeship on a C-Class freighter, the *Novocastrian* running the

Spiral Arm. There's no way this is a frigate, look at the size of the cargo hold."

"What the hell is she doing this far out of the space lanes?" Vegas asks.

"It's a ghost ship," Dr. Summers replies.

"You're not serious?" Michaels asks, turning to face Summers.

"The *Marie Céleste*," Dr. Summers continues, her voice shakes as she speaks. "She was found floating abandoned in the Atlantic Ocean by the *Dei Gratia*—she's a ghost ship."

"Now, hold on," Vegas says, turning to face the doctor. "What are you suggesting here, doc? That history is somehow repeating itself?"

"You're jumping to conclusions," Michaels says. "*Céleste* means star—it's a perfectly rational name for a French freighter."

"And *Dei Gratia*?" Dr. Summers counters, her eyes wide with fear. "How do you account for our name?"

"It's a coincidence," Vegas replies. "Nothing more. Shuttles have always been given Latin, Greek or Arabic names. We were named after some stupid tradition where kings and queens were said to rule by the grace of God. So what if some religious monarchist wants to keep a tradition alive, that means nothing to you and me."

"I'm telling you," Dr. Summers says. "This is wrong. We are in the wrong place, at the wrong time. We need to get out of here before we all die."

Michaels feels his blood run cold. The doctor's words are

ominous, as though she knows more than she's letting on.

"Wait a minute, Doc," Vegas replies in exasperation. "Nobody's died."

"Tell that to the crew of the *Céleste*," Dr. Summers insists.

GHOSTS

Sleet rains down on the *Dei Gratia*, lashing at the tripled-glazed windows, making it impossible to see the frozen plain stretching out before them. Landing lights fight off the dark of night, but even they seem unusually feeble. A faint glow on the horizon marks the coming dawn. Somewhere out there, Hubbard and Jacobs are exploring a derelict space freighter.

Flashes of lightning cut through the storm, arcing across the sky. Thunder rumbles overhead.

Vegas is lost deep in thought. Nobody on the bridge talks. The only sound is that of the heavy breathing of the astronauts coming in over the radio. Although it's only a few seconds, to Michaels it feels like an eternity before Vegas responds to Dr. Summers.

"We're going in. Get Phillips on the line. I'll take the call in my study and explain my decision to him. Michaels, you have the helm. All nonessential personnel are to clear the bridge. I want to know where that ship came from, how it ended up here, and what happened to its crew. Stay in direct contact with Hubbard. Have Jacobs remain outside the airlock ready to assist if the need arises."

No one speaks. Vegas elaborates on her orders.

"That's no ghost ship. It's real. I want answers, scientific answers. Michaels, you're going to get them for me. Understood?"

"Understood," Michaels replies. He likes it when Vegas is assertive. She inspires confidence.

Vegas walks out of the bridge. Her thin frame disappears into the bright-lit corridor. Michaels knows she's going to get roasted by Phillips, but she has the guts to make the hard calls, and the tenacity to live with them—that's why she's the away commander. He picks up a wireless headset with a microphone and makes eye contact with the communications officer, who nods in response, indicating the mic is live. Michaels isn't going to make the same mistake as Vegas and allow a quorum to form on the bridge. He intends to control communication from the outset. The coms officer points up at the speaker on the ceiling, and Michaels signals OK with his thumb up. He doesn't mind the others hearing the discussion, but he doesn't want them interrupting anything he says.

Dr. Summers leans against one of the consoles, staring at the screen and watching as Hubbard sets up a portable repeater outside the airlock. Hubbard continues working while the crew of the *Dei Gratia* debate the significance of the *Céleste,* talking to no one but himself. EVAs have that effect on people, Michaels notes. Working in a foreign environment is unnerving. Talking through each action settles the mind, helping it focus on the finer details. Hubbard keeps talking even though no one replies, not even Jacobs who's now at the base of the freighter. Hubbard knows they're there in the background and have muted the line, but it doesn't seem to bother him. He keeps talking. He's probably taking their silence as consent.

"I've got an oxyacetylene torch, grapple line, pickax... Helmet cam is set to broadcast to the booster. Should be picked up by the scout and relayed back to the *Dei Gratia*... Four hours of electrical juice. Recycling breathable oxygen. CO_2 scrubber is in the green. I am good for EVA extension."

"Hubbard, this is Michaels. We're reading your helmet cam. Image is coming through nice and clear."

"Roger that, Michaels."

"Vegas has you as GO for exploration of the *Céleste*, she's relaying this to the *Argo*. Jacobs, we're going to need you to return to the airlock and remain on standby."

"Fucking-A," Hubbard replies.

"You idiot," Jacobs mumbles from the ice, already stepping back onto the gantry.

The view from the camera helmet is fixed, resulting in the command group on the *Dei Gratia* seeing only in the direction of the faceplate on Hubbard's suit, while Hubbard himself is free to turn his head inside his helmet when looking around. It means Hubbard describes what he's doing or seeing a fraction of a second before he turns and brings the object into view.

"Airlock's tidy... No sign of conflict or confusion... Tell Vegas that's a negative on her fight... Four lightweight emergency suits on the rack... I see a pair of boots outside one of the lockers. Looks like there's been at least one surface EVA... Core drill... Mining laser... Sample bag containing rocks."

Hubbard holds up the frozen bag. The lights on his helmet

reflect off the plastic back at the camera, failing to clearly illuminate the contents.

"Is there any coral in there?" Michaels asks.

"Coral?" Hubbard replies in surprise.

"Yes, anything granular, almost cement-like, coarse and gritty."

Hubbard rotates the bag. His hands are clumsy in the thick gloves. He fumbles with the contents of the bag.

"Coral? On an ice planet?"

Michaels is silent, not sure if he's said too much. He noticed Vegas didn't inform the survey team about what happened to Johnson, and he feels obliged to follow her lead. In the back of his mind, he wonders about the morality of what he's condoning. Vegas said Johnson was injured, but that could mean anything. They have no idea his arm was torn off. They're going into harm's way without the knowledge of what they're facing. But what *is* out there in the darkness? Michaels can't even begin to describe what he saw through the panicked haze of a burning flare sticking into the ice. He swallows the lump in this throat.

"Could be, I guess," Hubbard says with a calm, nonchalant voice, taking one of the rocks out of the bag, "but it could just as easily be aerated igneous rock. Looks volcanic to me. From the weight, I'd say it's not pumice—too heavy. Feels more like granite formed within a gas pocket. Sorry, Michaels, no coral."

Michaels remains silent, his eyes picking out the subtle details he can see on the screen as Hubbard turns the rock in his hand.

"Do you think it's important? If you want, I can grab it on the way out."

"No. It's fine," Michaels replies. "Proceed forward."

The airlock is long and narrow, designed to allow small teams the ability to conduct egress and ingress as a group with ease. Hubbard walks slowly toward the inner door, his spotlight dances across the walls and floor as he moves. A shadow passes over the outer door behind him, causing the ambient light within the lock to narrow and darken. Michaels feels his heart skip a beat.

"Fuck," Hubbard cries, turning swiftly. He staggers, almost losing his footing.

Jacobs is standing in the doorway behind him. "What?" he asks innocently.

Hubbard laughs. "You scared me to death."

Jacobs looks around, seeing his shadow cast in the lock. He steps back, saying, "Sorry."

Hubbard turns his back on Jacobs. He moves cautiously forward, his spotlight illuminating the far door. He positions himself to one side of the door and pulls out his oxyacetylene torch. Even with his gloves on, it's clear his hands are shaking. Michaels glances up at Hubbard's vitals: heart rate 137 bpm.

"Take it easy," Michaels says. "Slow your breathing. You're burning through your O2."

In reality, short bursts of excitement like this won't have a material effect on his oxygen levels, but Michaels knows he needs to get Hubbard thinking about something practical, anything to get his mind off the fear of the moment.

The torch flares as a blue flame leaps from its tip. Hubbard adjusts the flame and cuts away the control panel beside the door. Spits of molten metal fall to the floor, glowing and seething, releasing methane gas from the frozen ice. Without oxygen, the methane won't combust, forming a low-hanging fog instead as it cools and condenses in the freezing cold atmosphere.

Over the suit microphone, the command group on the *Dei Gratia* hears the snap and hiss of the torch. The panel falls away, striking the metal hull beside Hubbard's feet with a resounding clang. Due to the thickness of the atmosphere, the noise is deep and resonant, reverberating through the airlock.

Michaels grimaces at the noise.

Jacobs speaks from behind Hubbard, saying, "Careful. You'll wake the dead."

"Very funny," Hubbard replies dryly.

Hubbard is using a standard procedure for forced entry, only normally the outer hatch would be closed first. He inserts a crank handle into the cog and pauses.

"What are we expecting on the other side?"

"Well, after almost two decades, I doubt there's a welcoming committee," Michaels replies.

Vegas walks back on the bridge. Michaels goes to hand her the headset, but she waves him off, taking a seat next to him. He's surprised by that, but he quickly realizes leaving him on point with Hubbard gives her a bit more objectivity.

"I mean, what's the pressure differential?" Hubbard asks. "I'm not going to blow myself out of the airlock, am I?"

"Negative," Michaels replies. "Good question. There's roughly four atmospheres around you. If anything, you'll be sucked in. Break the seal slowly. Given the age of the craft, my guess is she would have already equalized through a fine leak elsewhere."

"Is there any way to tell?" Hubbard asks.

"None."

"Fuck."

"I told you this was a bad idea," Jacobs adds.

Hubbard fights with the crank. For all his efforts, the inner door opens no more than a hair's breadth. He pauses, focusing on the tiny dark crack in the white inner door. Slowly, he waves his gloved hand in front of the crack, catching the light from his helmet as he does so.

"Thataboy," Michaels says. "I love the way you're conducting a precise empirical experiment to test for any pressure differential."

"Smartass," Hubbard replies, turning and working with the crank to open the door.

For his part, Michaels' comment was carefully calculated to defuse the tension. Vegas smiles. She knows.

It takes ten minutes before the inner door is wide enough for the astronaut to pass through. Hubbard is breathing hard as he finishes with the crank. Jacobs stands quietly behind him in the entrance to the airlock. Jacobs won't so much as take a step inside the craft, which Michaels finds curious. He could've helped, but he didn't, he just stood there watching from outside. Michaels can't fault him on that, but it's clear he's terrified about what could be lurking inside the abandoned craft.

Harris says something on the command deck in the *Dei Gratia*, but Michaels is so engrossed he barely hears his words. Harris points at the humidity reading on Hubbard's vitals and suit display.

"Can you check your environmental controls," Michaels says. "We're picking up a lot of humidity."

"Sweating like a pig," Hubbard replies. He stands in the doorway, looking into the pitch black darkness in the starship.

"You don't have to do this," Jacobs says.

"Oh," Hubbard replies. "I know, believe me, I know—but I have to."

He steps through the door. The corridor before him runs left to right. Hubbard turns one way and then the other, but his spotlight only illuminates the first fifteen to twenty feet, and even then only in a narrow band. Beyond that lies the darkness, giving the corridor seemingly eternal depth.

Michaels can't shake the feeling they're being watched. He can't explain why, and he knows it's irrational, but he feels as though someone is watching them, and not just Hubbard and Jacobs, but Vegas, Harris, Summers and himself. Michaels catches some movement out of the corner of his eye, and feels compelled to turn and look at the open doorway leading to the bridge. There's no one there, and Michaels feels stupid when Summers and Vegas follow his gaze and then look to him for some kind of explanation. He isn't sure what he was looking for, but he felt as though someone was standing there watching them just moments ago.

"Which way?" Hubbard asks, snapping him back to reality.

Harris has the schematics of C-Class freighters displayed on an adjacent screen.

Looking at the floor plan, Michaels says, "The bridge is two floors up, and to your left. Engineering is about a hundred feet to your right. Right in front of you there should be a hatch leading to the cargo hold."

"I don't see any hatch," Hubbard replies.

"Don't worry about it," Michaels says. "We're working off general schematics for this class. There's bound to be some differences between them, but the overall layout should be the same. There should be shift quarters to your left."

Hubbard turns and walks into the pitch black darkness.

Michaels feels as though he's back out on the ice with Johnson. He remembers how the creatures attacked from behind, slashing at the two of them before peeling away into the shadows, never venturing into the light. To his mind, darkness is an invitation. His hands tremble as he watches the video feed coming in from Hubbard.

Hubbard's breathing is ragged and hoarse. Although he's wearing an exoskeleton to take the edge off the gravity, he seems to be laboring. His inhalations sound like a wheeze, as though he has hay fever, while his exhalations have a distinct rasp, as though his lungs are being completely emptied. In the eerie silence within the derelict, Hubbard's hoarse breathing adds to the terror.

The darkness is oppressive, closing in around the lone astronaut. Michaels feels as though he's walking through the abandoned corridor with Hubbard.

Hubbard turns. His spotlights catch a glimpse of what should be a familiar, friendly setting: the gritty, non-slip flooring, handholds for zero-g, small signs marking access points to wiring and plumbing. Perhaps that's what scares Michaels the most. Hubbard could be walking through the darkened interior of the *Dei Gratia*.

Hubbard pauses and looks back. Soft light spills onto the dark floor, marking the hatchway twenty feet behind him.

"How are you doing?" Michaels asks.

"I'm good."

Hubbard turns and continues down the corridor. The floor and walls are covered in a fine sprinkling of ice, glittering in the spotlights. There are junction boxes on the walls, signs for the Mess and the Infirmary, the ceiling lighting strips are darkened and powerless. Hubbard steps into one of the rooms.

"Should be a general crew berth," Michaels says, mentally correlating Hubbard's progress through the *Céleste* with the schematic Harris has displayed on a secondary monitor. "Somewhere for shift workers to bed down without heading back to the dorm."

"Look at this," Hubbard says, turning toward a table so both the spotlights and the camera focus on a cup and plate. A half-eaten doughnut sits abandoned on a plastic plate. There are crumbs on the table. The coffee mug is almost full. Hubbard picks up the cup and holds it so the camera can see the murky frozen contents. He turns the coffee cup upside down, watching as the solidified coffee stays in place.

"Whatever happened here," he says, "it happened quickly—in the middle of the day, and while they were resting. They left everything. Must have been in a hurry."

"Could it have been a fire?" Michaels asks.

"Negative," Hubbard replies, looking up at the clean ceiling. "No sign of smoke damage, at least not here."

"Where are the bodies?" Jacobs asks. He must be watching Hubbard's progress from outside the *Céleste* on his wrist monitor.

"You're not helping," Michaels replies.

Jacobs is silent.

Hubbard ignores them, examining a cot in the berth. Blankets and sheets lay crumpled together, as though the occupant woke briefly to go to the bathroom. He reaches out and touches the blanket with his gloved hand.

"Rock solid... like a goddamn fossil."

Michaels catches movement on the edge of the camera feed at roughly the same time as Hubbard—a subtle flicker in the blind spot obscured by the edge of his helmet and just beyond the camera lens.

Hubbard turns. Michaels feels his heart race. In his panic, Hubbard knocks something metallic across the darkened floor. The crash of a steel panel falling to the frozen floor seems to wake the dead. A flash of light catches his camera, blinding the distant view on the bridge of the *Dei Gratia*. For Michaels, the blur of motion is terrifying, eerily reminiscent of the way Johnson was attacked on the windswept, icy plain. He feels his body stiffen, on the verge of cramping as he flexes, trying not to jump at the sight before him.

"What the hell?" Hubbard cries, yelling into his microphone.

Another astronaut peers back at Hubbard from not more than three feet away. The glare of the astronaut's spotlights makes it difficult to resolve any features beyond the faceplate. Michaels leaps forward, reaching out with his hand and touching at the astronaut on the screen, trying to see the mission patch on the his shoulder in a vain attempt to identify him, but there's too much motion. It's then Michaels notices Hubbard waving. He's laughing. There, staring back at him, is his own reflection, mirroring his every move.

Hubbard laughs.

"You dumb fuck," Jacobs says from outside the *Céleste*, watching the same feed as Michaels.

Hubbard shakes his head, rocking both his helmet and the camera. Light reflects off the floor-to-ceiling mirror, highlighting the wall behind him. The reflection drifts with his motion.

Something moves.

Something other than the shadows cast by his space suit.

Someone's behind him, caught for a fleeting moment along with his reflection.

Hubbard spins around, but in the heavy gravity, he loses his footing and falls backwards against the mirror. Glass shatters, exploding outward and showering the floor. Tiny bits of mirror scatter across the slick surface like sparks from a welder. Hubbard falls awkwardly and cries out in pain. A dark shape flees the room, darting out into the corridor.

"Are you OK?" Michaels asks.

Hubbard is slow to respond. He grimaces in pain.

"I think I've sprained my wrist. Hurts like a mo-fo."

He's breathing heavily.

"Did you guys see that?" he asks. "Tell me you saw that."

"I've got it," Harris replies, although Michaels knows Hubbard can't hear anyone else on the bridge.

"Stay where you are," Michaels says to Hubbard as Harris brings up a video clip on the secondary monitor. He steps through the frames in slow motion. Splinters of glass ricochet slowly off the floor during the replay, causing light to scatter around the astronaut as he falls. A gloved hand reaches out as the floor twists sideways.

"There," says Vegas, tapping the screen as they watch the grainy image in the half-light. Although Hubbard's motion in turning to face the creature was replayed at quarter speed, the frame-blur makes it impossible to catch anything beyond a dark silhouette. The creature was sneaking around behind him, and appears surprised by Hubbard's sudden motion. It bolted toward the door as the camera and spotlights rippled across the floor. Harris rewinds and replays one short section, catching a brief flicker that flashes before them. Locking in on one frame, he enhances the clearest of the images.

"Looks to be roughly four feet in height," Vegas says. "What are those long white barbs in the head? Teeth?"

"What's happening?" Hubbard whispers. "What was that? Should I go after it?"

"No," Michaels replies emphatically, not looking for confirmation from anyone. "Give us a moment."

"Oh, fine," Hubbard replies, getting to his feet. "Take your sweet fucking time. Nothing to see here. Just an astronaut freaking the fuck out!"

Hubbard faces the doorway, illuminating it with his spotlights. The live video stream is washed out as a flare is lit. Within seconds, smoke begins pouring from the red flare. Hubbard holds it at arm's length in a feeble show of defense. The room appears blood red, with long shadows stretching away from the flare. The smoke drifts in front of the camera, reducing the visibility of the crew onboard the *Dei Gratia*.

"Is this what you saw?" Vegas says to Michaels, tapping the secondary monitor and pulling his eyes away from the main screen.

Michaels reaches up and mutes his microphone. "I think so."

"Get him out of there," Vegas says. "We've seen enough."

"Roger that," Dr. Summers says.

"Hubbard," Michaels says, switching his microphone back on. "Time to leave. Meet up with Jacobs and get back to the *Dei Gratia*. That's an order."

"You're kidding me, right?" Hubbard replies, apparently

finding his courage and peering around the corner into the darkness. "Don't you want to know what that thing was?"

Hubbard tosses the flare out into the hallway. The brilliance of the burning phosphorous shines like a shooting star as it skids across the floor, bathing the corridor in brilliant red light. Smoke billows to the ceiling, a burning pillar streaming away from the flare. A thin haze hangs in the air.

Michaels looks at Vegas. She nods. There's an unspoken understanding between them, a trust that says more than either of them could express at that moment. Michaels knows instinctively that she wants him to tell Hubbard about what happened by the thermal pools.

"Listen," Michaels says, "Johnson and I were attacked by these creatures. Johnson lost his arm. They ripped it off. Now is not the time for bravado."

"I thought you were a scientist?" Hubbard replies, his voice breaking up as he speaks. He leaves the sleeping berth and begins creeping along the hallway, moving away from the airlock, keeping his back against the wall. "Aren't you curious? I mean, this is life, right? This is alien life. We've found it! This is the Holy Grail. We've hit the *goddamn* jackpot!"

"This isn't a game show," Michaels answers. "Best we understand it, these things are wild animals. Something akin to a lion, or a tiger. They're not to be messed with. As it is, we've pushed things too far. They could interpret your EVA as a hostile act, intruding on their territory. You don't want to provoke an attack."

"Look at that," Hubbard says, ignoring him.

Hubbard tilts his helmet down toward his feet so the camera catches the ice crystals glistening in his spotlights. There are footsteps leading down the corridor. "Bipeds! What are the odds? And look at the gait, the instep, five toes on each foot. Damn, it's like seeing a child's footprint on a sandy beach."

The flare flickers on the ground behind him.

Vegas waves at Michaels, signaling for him to give her the headset. He rips it off, catching the soft cartilage on his ear as the chrome frame flexes, leaving a throbbing welt. The pain anchors his mind in the moment.

Vegas slips the headset neatly over her ears, without upsetting the tight strands of hair pulled back into a ponytail.

"Hubbard," she says. "These creatures are not to be trifled with. You need to get out of there while you still can."

"Vegas?" Hubbard replies. He seems genuinely surprised to hear directly from her. "Come on. Don't tell me you're afraid of the dark?"

"I'm afraid of what's in the dark," Vegas says. "This isn't some figment of your imagination, some childhood monster lurking under the bed. These creatures are real. They're vicious."

On the screen, Hubbard stops walking. He looks back, past the flare and toward the dim light spilling across the corridor in the distance. A faint smudge of light marks the airlock. Somehow, it seems as though by facing that direction he's addressing them personally as he speaks.

"Listen, Vegas. I know those things attacked Johnson, but have you stopped and considered they didn't attack Michaels? Doesn't that strike you as strange? And they didn't kill either of them. They both lived."

Vegas replies with a surprisingly calm tone as she says, "They tore off his *fucking* arm." Her soft, feminine voice shakes Michaels. It's the juxtaposition—the stark contrast of her tone combined with such a coarse term. It shouldn't surprise him. Vegas is in command of a mining shuttle. Miners aren't renowned for their subtlety, and neither is she. He's heard her swear before, but her soft voice takes him off guard. Rather than shouting at Hubbard, she's appealing to reason.

"I know. I know," Hubbard says as he turns away from the airlock and continues to inch down the corridor.

The ruddy light given off by the flare casts long, dark shadows down the hallway, lighting up Hubbard's spacesuit in a ghostly silhouette.

Jacobs speaks from outside the airlock. "Will you just stop and listen to her, you idiot? For once in your life, don't be so *goddamn* stubborn."

Hubbard laughs, saying, "Harris. I know you're there somewhere, listening in the background. How do I get to the bridge? I'm not coming all this way to turn back at the first sign of trouble. Did you see that thing scamper? It was more afraid of me than I was of it. That was just a bump in the dark, nothing more, nothing to panic about."

"Hubbard," Vegas says, her voice stern.

The storm eases for a moment, allowing Hubbard's reply to come through clearly.

"I want answers. I want to know what those things are. I want to know why the captain of the *Céleste* landed a freighter on this *godforsaken* icy rock. He could have stayed in orbit and used shuttles to commute. He must have known something we don't. And where the hell did he go? Where is everybody? What happened to the crew?"

"They're dead!" Dr. Summers yells from the bridge of the *Dei Gratia*, loud enough to be picked up by the microphone. "They're all dead! Don't you get that? If you don't get out of there, you'll die too."

"Relax, Doc," Hubbard says. "Pop some Valium for me."

No one on the *Dei Gratia* speaks. Vegas shakes her head. Dr. Summers cradles a cup of coffee in her hand. At first, Michaels assumes she's warming her fingers, but she's trying to stop them shaking. She sips gingerly at the coffee, trying to hide her panic. Michaels is surprised. Given her medical training, he didn't expect her to be so rattled.

As Hubbard pushes on, the light from the flare fades. The corridor runs the length of the ship, covering at least a quarter mile, and before long the flare is nothing but a distant glimmer of light, slowly flickering and fading as it burns out.

Hubbard's breathing hard, which is unusual as he's using an exoskeleton like the one Michaels and Johnson wore during their survey of the thermal pools. Michaels wonders if he's powered down to save his battery, or if he prefers the struggle. Some of the miners are like that, relishing the opportunity to exercise their muscles in a gravity field. He listens carefully and notices Hubbard's breathing is out of sync with his pace. Michaels himself uses that strategy when running long distance on the treadmill, as it helps avoid the stitch while exercising, but with Hubbard it doesn't seem deliberate. It has to be fear. Hubbard has a reputation as an adrenaline junkie, but is this too much for him?

The twin spotlights on either side of Hubbard's helmet are no match for the darkness. They briefly light up the walls and illuminate darkened doorways as the lone astronaut walks slowly on. Michaels finds his muscles clenching, expecting something to jump out of the shadows at Hubbard. The attack on the ice came without warning, and flashes of that moment continue to replay in his mind as he watches the grainy footage coming in from the *Céleste*. Now they've established there's at least one creature inside the *Céleste* with Hubbard, it would be foolish to assume there aren't more. Perhaps they hunt in packs, as wolves do on Earth. Michaels starts to say something but words are pointless. Hubbard has made up his mind. All any of them can do is watch and hope.

"The *Argo* is now over the horizon," Harris says, turning to Vegas. "Two hours until AOS."

AOS—acquisition of signal. The crew of the *Dei Gratia* are on their own until the mothership passes overhead again. Michaels feels uneasy with the forced isolation. Vegas sits on the edge of the nav desk. She sighs, gesturing to the screen. Like Michaels, she's helpless—resigned to watching Hubbard walk deeper into the *Céleste*.

"What do we do if one of those things attacks him?" Harris asks.

It's precisely what Michaels wants to ask, but he doesn't want to be the one to verbalize their fears. He suspects he already knows the answer Vegas will give: Hubbard is on his own.

Vegas looks at Harris, and with her microphone muted, she says, "Whatever happens, this is by his choice. There's nothing we can do."

Hubbard pauses, looking back briefly into the darkness as the flare finally dies. The airlock is no longer visible. The darkened interior of the ship looks more like a tomb than a freighter.

He turns and walks on until his spotlights illuminate a series of lifts leading to the other floors.

"Without power, I'm going to have to use the access hatch," Hubbard says, breaking his uncomfortable silence with the *Dei Gratia*. Neither side has spoken since he defied Vegas. He asks, "How far to the bridge?"

Harris holds up two fingers.

"Two floors," Vegas says, switching her microphone back to broadcast.

"See, I knew you were still there," Hubbard says, pulling a maintenance hatch off the wall.

"He's not going to fit," Harris says. "Those ducts are designed for a single engineer. They're tight at the best of times. It'll be impossible to get inside wearing a spacesuit, let alone climb the ladder."

"Harris says you won't fit," Vegas says, passing the message along. "You're too bulky."

Hubbard puts the hatch to one side. He leans the steel panel against the wall but it slips and crashes to the floor. The explosion of sound is surprisingly loud. Hubbard jumps at the noise.

Michaels shakes his head. "This is not going to end well."

"You won't fit," Jacobs cries, speaking over the radio from outside the craft. "That shaft is too narrow. You'll die in there."

"You optimist," Hubbard replies. "If I lose the exoskeleton and the EVA pack, I'll fit. The shaft should run from steerage to the observation deck."

"Haven't you seen this movie?" Jacobs asks. "Because I have. This is the scene where a *goddamn* face-hugger jumps out at you and its acid eats through your helmet! Get out of there, you idiot!"

Hubbard laughs.

From the safety of the command deck on the *Dei Gratia*, Michaels watches as Hubbard unclips the mechanical harness that provides powered assistance when walking and lifting in heavy gravity.

"I'm serious, man," Jacobs adds. "You're freaking me out."

"You've seen too many movies," Hubbard replies. "And besides, they never get the leading man."

Harris taps his watch and signals with two fingers. Vegas takes the hint.

"Harris says you've got two minutes' oxygen without your EVA pack on. Just what the hell are you proposing to do without life support?"

Hubbard is breathing hard as he unclips the shoulder straps and swings the pack around to one side, leaning it against the wall.

"Hubbard?"

On the monitor, they watch as Hubbard reaches into the puncture repair kit in the pocket below his right knee. He pulls out a small length of dual tubing, where the incoming and outgoing supply lines lie side by side. He struggles, saying, "Suits were designed for buddy-breathing."

Michaels notes his sentence is clipped, highlighting the stress he's under. Dr. Summers seems to notice as well. She leans forward, watching the subtleties in his motion.

Hubbard pulls on the tube. Its compact, accordion-like structure allows it to stretch to a length of three feet. He attaches one end to the front plate on his suit and the other to the EVA pack, and begins purging the lines and pressurizing the buddy breathing apparatus.

Harris holds his fingers in the shape of a zero, indicating how much time's remaining. Two minutes have passed since Hubbard disconnected from the EVA pack. Hubbard is breathing heavily, sucking in hard as his lungs seek oxygen.

He fights with the controls on his wrist computer. Michaels knows the CO_2 will be building up in his suit. No one speaks. The last thing he needs is to be distracted. Hubbard's fingers look bulky and clumsy in his gloves. He stabs at the digital controls. In the silence, a soft hiss announces the flow of oxygen and the processing of CO_2.

Michaels breathes a sigh of relief, noting that Harris, Summers, and Vegas have been holding their breath as well.

"You are one persistent son of a bitch," Vegas says.

Hubbard just laughs.

"I'm telling ya," he replies. "Ain't no little green dwarf alien going to mess with the Big Dog... Big Dog's gonna get him some answers."

Although Michaels thinks Hubbard is reckless, acting out of pride, he can't help but admire the man's tenacity. A lesser man would have never set foot in the airlock, let alone have gone on after the first encounter. Perhaps Hubbard's right. They need answers. What are they going to do otherwise? Retreat into orbit? And then what? Run like a dog with its tail between its legs? As harsh and unforgiving as this planet is—with lightning storms raging across the surface and cyclonic winds at the equator—there's life down here. Life! This frozen wasteland is the most unlikely place Michaels can think of to find life beyond Earth, but here it was, and it demanded investigation.

"This is important," Hubbard says, "more important than any of us. We have a duty to go on."

Michaels dares to consider that Hubbard might be right. He too feels they have a duty to find out all they can about the lifeforms on this planet—and that another starship arrived decades before them only heightens the sense of importance in unraveling this mystery. Michaels doesn't want to say anything to the others, but secretly he admires Hubbard's courage.

Michaels isn't a coward, and yet he doubts he would have gone on board the abandoned freighter, but like Hubbard, he desperately wants to know why it's there. What did the crew of the *Céleste* find? What did they uncover in the ice? Most important of all, what mistakes did they make? And how can the crew of the *Dei Gratia* avoid the same fate? Hubbard's right. They need to get to the bridge and get some answers.

Harris is ever the professional. He speaks into a secondary microphone, saying, "That suit and life support kit is at least a hundred and twenty pounds in a standard gravity."

Hubbard squeezes through the maintenance hatch, pulling the EVA pack behind him as Harris continues.

"Without your assisters, it's gonna feel like one-sixty to one-eighty, which is like dragging a dead body."

That probably isn't the best analogy.

The helmet camera struggles with auto-focus at such close range in the elevator shaft. Bare sheet metal moves in and out of focus. The rungs set into the bulkhead knock into Hubbard's helmet as he begins to climb. He grimaces as he's using his sore hand to hold on to the ladder.

Harris turns off his microphone and speaks to Vegas, saying, "With an injured hand and one arm dragging that pack, he's going to have to use his legs to climb. It's going to be a long, slow ascent."

During the climb, Hubbard doesn't talk. From the grunts and groans, they can tell he's struggling. The narrow conduit is barely wide enough for him in his bulky suit. His helmet bangs against the rungs in front of him and the sheet metal behind him as he pushes against the wall for leverage.

"He is one stubborn son of a bitch," Harris mutters.

The view on the screen is skewed sideways, as Hubbard's right shoulder hangs down under the weight of the EVA pack. Hubbard wedges his back against the wall and shimmies upwards. At times, he pauses, with both arms by his side as he leans against the wall and catches his breath.

Harris counts with his fingers. He notices Michaels staring at him curiously.

"Five rungs per floor. He's covered nine. He should be almost level with the upper deck. Only six to go."

"Harris says you're doing well," Vegas says to Hubbard. "Six rungs to go."

Hubbard drags himself up another rung, saying, "Sweat in my eyes... Visor's fogging up... Can't see a goddamn thing."

Vegas replies. "You're running on quarter power in buddy-mode. Once you hook up the EVA pack again your suit will extract the humidity."

Hubbard's breathing is shallow and quick, coming in pants with the exertion of climbing higher.

"He could get stuck in there," Michaels notes. No one seems pleased with his observation. They look at him as though he's said something to curse the man.

As Hubbard rests, the officers on the bridge of the *Dei Gratia* hear a noise over the communication link, a faint sound like that of a cat scratching at a door.

"Are you hearing that?" Vegas asks.

Hubbard shifts his weight. He's trying to look down, but in the confines of the shaft, his helmet restricts his vision.

"Can't see the hatch. Wait, there's a shadow. Looks like someone wants to keep me company. Do you think they'll let me keep him as a pet?"

Hubbard laughs. No one replies. No one else thinks that's funny.

Michaels feels panicked. He can't believe how blithely Hubbard is treating the situation, trapped in a claustrophobic shaft with an alien scurrying around below. The thought of being attacked terrifies Michaels, and he finds himself looking around the command deck on the *Dei Gratia* to assure himself he's safe from those dark monsters that struck on the icy plain.

Harris closes the doors to the bridge, probably to keep curious crewmembers from peeking, but Michaels can't help wonder if Harris feels a little paranoid too. He doubts it. Harris moves with professionalism and precision. His crew cut hair and sharp-pressed uniform reflect his military past.

Summers is a wreck. Her eyes are bloodshot. Her hair is unkempt. She doesn't look like the same person that walked him up to the bridge barely an hour before. Their eyes meet and he understands. Michaels feels the same way.

Michaels has an irrational compulsion to check his blind spots, as if somehow he's being watched even though his back is against a console on the bulkhead. He turns anyway, reassuring himself there's nothing there. Vegas notices his motion, but nothing seems to register, she's preoccupied with Hubbard. Michaels wonders about the dynamic on the bridge, whether he and Summers would be better suited to handling the stress if Vegas and Harris weren't so outwardly calm. It seems as though they are an emotional counterbalance amidst the tension.

The creature thrashes around in the narrow space at the bottom of the ladder.

"I think I'll call him George," Hubbard says.

"I think George wants you to move along," Vegas replies coldly.

"Yep."

"Whatever you do," Vegas adds, "don't lose your grip on that EVA pack."

"Yep."

Hubbard continues to climb.

"His heart is hitting a hundred and eighty beats per minute," Dr. Summers says, her voice breaking in a quiver as she speaks.

"Doc says you need to slow down," Vegas says. "Your heart's working overtime."

"Yep," is the exhausted reply.

Hubbard struggles on at the same pace.

"He should be coming up on the hatch," Harris says.

"Can you see the hatch?" Vegas asks.

"I think I felt the rim hit the side of my helmet as I came up that last rung," Hubbard replies. He pushes on to another rung and says, "There's something digging into my upper back. That must be the lever."

They can hear him reaching around with his left arm as he leans to one side. The acoustics in the frozen maintenance shaft amplify even the slightest noise.

"Damn thing is stuck."

Dr. Summers bites at her nails. She's a wreck.

Grunting, Hubbard puts his strength into gaining some leverage on the frozen handle. The handle gives and the hatch falls open, tumbling out into the upper hallway with a loud clang. Summers jumps at the sound.

Leaning back against the side of the shaft, Hubbard uses one hand to pull out a flare. He pushes the tip of the flare into the doorjamb, forcing it between the two sheets of metal lining the shaft. He fumbles with the flare, unable to use his other hand. Finally, the top twists off the flare and a brilliant red light cuts through the darkness. Smoke billows up the shaft.

Hubbard tosses the flare into the hallway. He's panting hard with the exertion. Slowly, he pushes off with his feet, pushing his upper torso out onto the floor. He's face down and slightly to one side, giving the crew on the *Dei Gratia* an oblique view of the hallway. The flare burns somewhere out of sight, casting blood red hues across the floor. The hallway's empty. In the shadows, Michaels can make out the entrance to the bridge.

"He's made it," Michaels says, subconsciously ignoring the reality that Hubbard has to retrace his steps to leave the *Céleste*. At best, he's halfway.

"You're doing great, Hubbard," Vegas says, clearly relieved he's made it to the bridge.

Hubbard's helmet tilts, giving them a view of the hatchway behind him as he fights to pull himself onto the floor. His legs are still inside the shaft and his right arm is partially pinned beneath his suit. He lies still for a moment, catching his breath.

"Be careful you don't snag your air line," Vegas says. "You're going to need that to get back down."

"Roger that."

They watch as Hubbard wriggles, struggling to get onto the floor. They can see his gloved hand holding the strap of the EVA pack. His life support system is still well within the shaft.

"My boot's caught on one of the rungs."

Hubbard twists his body, trying to free his boot.

"Watch that air line," Vegas reiterates.

"Pack weighs a ton," Hubbard grunts, pulling on the strap as he tries to shift the EVA unit. On the screen, the officers can just see the edge of the pack coming level with the floor. It must be pressing against his pinned leg. Hubbard's in an awkward position, and the weight of his suit works against him.

"Gravity sucks," he says, almost losing his grip on the pack.

"Slow things down," Vegas says. "Be methodical. Take your

time."

"Easy for you to say," Hubbard complains, still lying on one side. "FUUUUCK!!!"

The sound of the EVA pack falling down the shaft drowns out the other swear words Hubbard yells. His suit automatically registers the loss of pressure in the buddy-breathing interface and closes the ports to the now torn air line.

Dr. Summers gasps. She places her hand over her mouth in horror.

Vegas reacts immediately, speaking to Harris. "Cut the audio. Get me Jacobs."

Michaels understands what she's doing. By muting Hubbard she can talk directly with Jacobs without the need to talk over the top of a man on the verge of dying.

"Jacobs. I need you to get to Hubbard. You're going to have to buddy with him. We'll get a second scout craft out to assist you. Stay in place. We'll come to you."

There's no reply, and for a moment the look on her face suggests she thinks Harris has cut both lines of communication.

"Jacobs?"

"Yeah, I read you," is the reluctant reply. "Shit. How the hell did I end up with Hubbard?"

"Get in there," Vegas yells.

"I'm on my way."

Harris cuts in on the transmission, saying, "Be careful, there's at least one creature on the landing."

"I know. I know," Jacobs replies, running through the darkness. The sound of his boots pounding on the floor reverberates through the hallway.

Although they can't hear what Hubbard's saying, his frantic scrambling is visible on screen, telling them all they need to know. Hubbard is fighting to squeeze back into the shaft. He's pushing himself backwards, maneuvering his bulky space suit to climb back down. Hubbard is inside the shaft when Harris brings the audio back up. He's wheezing as he climbs down the ladder rungs.

"Jacobs is on his way," Vegas barks.

Harris puts the secondary feed from Jacobs' helmet camera on another screen. Jacobs is holding a flare out in front of him. In the darkness, it's impossible to tell how fast he's moving, but the sound of his boots and his heavy breathing makes it clear he's running hard. The glare from the flare and the billowing smoke obscures the camera view.

"Better fucking hurry," Hubbard cries, struggling down the rungs inside the bulkhead.

Harris has started a timer.

"How long?" Hubbard asks. He knows the drill. He isn't stupid. He knows his chances of survival are slim. The timer has already passed down to less than a minute. In under sixty seconds, the CO_2 in his suit will begin to reach dangerous levels.

Vegas ignores Hubbard, saying, "You're going to be fine. Slow your breathing and keep moving."

"Roger that. I'm going to—"

Hubbard slips and falls.

His helmet rebounds off several of the rungs as he struggles to arrest his fall. The shaft begins in the cargo hold, so there's a danger he may fall past the landing Jacobs is running towards. Hubbard's gloved hands flail about madly grabbing for the rungs.

"Ah, shit!" Hubbard cries, coming to a stop. His helmet is on a chaotic angle, facing up through the shaft. A thin crack runs through his visor. "I am fucked. I am so fucked."

"What happened?" Vegas demands.

"Caught my leg."

Hubbard is struggling to speak.

"I think I've broken my lower leg. *Goddamn* knee is jammed in between one of the rungs and the wall. Stings like a mo-fo."

Harris makes the sign of a zero with his hand. Hubbard is out of usable air in his suit.

"How far did you fall?" Vegas asks.

"I'm fucked," Hubbard replies. His voice sounds distant, dazed.

"Jacobs. How far away are you?"

Jacobs is panting as he says, "Just coming up on the shaft."

On the secondary monitor, the team watches as Jacobs runs up to the open hatchway. He tosses his flare on the ground and leans inside the shaft to have a look. The spotlights on the side of his helmet illuminate the access way, revealing Hubbard jammed just above the floor.

"I see you, buddy." Jacobs may have cursed Hubbard before, but Michaels can sense the camaraderie kicking in with the desire to save his friend's life. Miners are renowned for their vulgarity and trash-talk, but when disaster strikes they're brothers.

Hubbard doesn't reply, but the officers on the *Dei Gratia* can hear them both breathing.

"Can you reach him?" Vegas asks.

"Not without shedding the exoskeleton," Jacobs replies. "Gonna have to pull off my EVA pack as well."

"Don't leave me here," Hubbard whispers.

"We're not going to leave you," Vegas replies.

"We're losing him," Dr. Summers says softly. "His heartbeat is erratic."

"Don't leave me here as a goddamn popsicle," Hubbard pleads. He's crying. The bravado in his voice is replaced by a tremor.

On the secondary monitor, the crew watch as Hubbard's left hand reaches down toward Jacobs. For his part, Jacobs is struggling to unclip his exoskeleton.

"Don't leave me," Hubbard repeats. "Don't let me die alone."

There's something in his voice, a resignation, and Michaels knows Hubbard's right. He isn't going to make it out of the *Céleste* alive. Jacobs seems to realize that as well. He stops what he's doing and reaches up, holding the dying man's hand. On the bridge of the

Dei Gratia, the crew watch as Jacobs squeezes the gloved hand reaching down for him.

For a few seconds, there's silence.

Michaels wipes a tear from his eye.

"I'm sorry," is all Dr. Summers can bring herself to say. The flat lines next to Hubbard's vital signs tell them he's dead. Jacobs must feel the change as Hubbard's life slips away. He lets go of the gloved hand and steps back. Behind him, his flare flickers and fades, slowly dying, surrendering to the darkness.

QUESTIONS

Dr. Summers cries. Vegas looks pale. Harris is tightlipped. Michaels is shaking. He tries to hide his fear by folding his arms, but he's sure the others have noticed. No one speaks. Vegas pulls the headset off, tossing it on the navigation console in disgust. By disconnecting, she's opened the channel to the bridge mic, meaning Jacobs will hear everything that's said by the command group.

Over the radio, Jacobs asks, "Do you want me to get him down from there?"

"Negative," Vegas replies. "Pull out."

Dr. Summers begins, "But you said–"

"I KNOW WHAT I SAID," Vegas snaps. She pauses, breathing deeply. With her head tilted and her eyes shut tight, she pinches the bridge of her nose, composing herself as she repeats, "I know what I said." There's capitulation in her voice. "I know," she adds feebly. Michaels swallows the lump in his throat. He slumps on the edge of the communications console feeling helpless—inadequate. For all his scientific knowledge, his years of training, nothing has prepared him for this.

Summers sobs quietly.

"So I just leave him?" Jacobs asks. His voice is inquisitive, not accusative. He seems genuinely surprised by Vegas, particularly given Hubbard's expressed last wish. Michaels wonders if it's guilt. Jacobs sounds detached, almost clinical, but that's probably due to the electronic waves that link them across the miles. Had Jacobs gone in there with Hubbard, things might have been different. That must play on his mind, and yet given what happened to Johnson on the windswept plains by the thermal pools, there is another scenario that's equally likely: there could be two bodies on that derelict spaceship, not one.

Hubbard's death was an accident. Had Jacobs been there, they could have gone on to run into a swarm of the creatures just as Michaels and Johnson had. In his fearful imagination, Michaels wonders if the long abandoned derelict has become a home for these creatures. Given Hubbard's encounter within twenty feet of the airlock, that's not a bad assumption.

Harris switches monitors, putting Jacobs on the main screen but leaving Hubbard's camera displayed on the secondary monitor. The spotlights on Hubbard's helmet illuminate the shaft, revealing ladder rungs reaching up into the darkness.

"It's not worth the risk," is all Vegas can say in response to Jacobs. As much as Michaels hates to admit it, she's right.

Jacobs adjusts his exoskeleton. Behind him, the flare lying on the floor dies, leaving him alone in the dark with his helmet-mounted spotlights flickering over the frozen corridor.

"He should light another flare," Michaels says.

"Michaels recommends you use another flare," Vegas says, relaying the advice without emotion, even though Jacobs can hear him fine. That she repeated Michaels makes it obvious she's emotionally spent. Even Harris is rattled.

"Copy that."

They watch as Jacobs strikes another flare and begins making his way back down the corridor to the airlock. He holds the flare to one side, giving both himself and the crew on the *Dei Gratia* a good view of the hallway as smoke billows toward the ice covered ceiling.

No one speaks. Jacobs isn't as chatty as Hubbard, and the command group on the bridge is in shock.

Jacobs is more weary than Hubbard. As he approaches the various darkened doorways, he crosses to the far side of the corridor, giving them a wide berth. He approaches the airlock, but not before taking one last glance down the hallway into the murky black void. Michaels wonders what he's thinking. He's probably offering a silent farewell to Hubbard, one last goodbye.

Jacobs backs out of the airlock, clearly not wanting to turn his back on the darkness.

Outside, the storm has fallen, darkening the sky. The wind picks up, making it difficult for Jacobs to descend to the ice below. The gantry flexes in the storm, twisting as gusts buffet the flimsy structure.

Michaels stares at the secondary monitor still receiving the live feed from Hubbard's helmet camera. Even without the EVA pack, his spotlights will probably last for the best part of an hour before the cold sets in and his battery power fades. In that moment, Michaels isn't sure what he's thinking. He gazes at the empty shaft and the dark opening on the next floor. He feels numb, dazed by the loss of Hubbard.

The helmet rocks gently.

"Hey, he's alive. Hubbard's still alive!"

They're his words, but it feels as though someone else has spoken them. His eyes glance down at the vital signs from the suit's telemetry readings. Flat lines stretch out next to the metrics for heartbeat and respiration.

"The suit must have been damaged in the fall," Dr. Summers says. "Maybe the lifeline didn't sever." Like Michaels, her first reaction is to think the telemetry readings are in error. Hubbard's spacesuit took the brunt of the impact as he fell. It's entirely plausible telemetry was knocked offline.

The helmet continues to rock. From the motion, it appears as though Hubbard's nodding in agreement, but his helmet rests on his shoulders, not his neck. Any movement Hubbard makes with his neck would go unnoticed in the helmet.

"He's trying to right himself," Michaels says, watching as Hubbard appears to arch his back in the tight confines of the shaft.

Green claws appear on the edge of the screen, scratching at the visor.

Michaels feels sick. Summers gasps. Harris reaches to kill the video feed.

"Don't," Michaels calls out, anticipating his action.

He has to see this. He has to learn from this encounter regardless of how macabre it might be. Humanity has wondered for centuries about First Contact. From such frivolous speculation as sci-fi movies, to serious scientific research like SETI, there had been considerable mental effort devoted to understanding an encounter with extraterrestrial life, and here it is, only it doesn't fit expectations. Michaels doesn't want to watch, but he has to. Sitting there, he feels as though a grave is being desecrated. The creature begins to shake the helmet with vigor.

"What is it doing?" Dr. Summers gasps.

Vegas has her hand over her mouth. As science officer, Michaels feels compelled to provide some commentary.

"Ah, it's recognizing the suit as some kind of shell—with the frail human animal hidden safely inside. The alien's trying to pry off the helmet, but it doesn't understand the use of a circular collar as a locking mechanism."

"You think it's trying to take his helmet off?" Vegas asks.

"It wants to, but it's rocking rather than twisting. Its motion is reminiscent of a crow solving a problem by trial and error." For Michaels, this behavior confirms something he suspected out on the ice, "They're brutes, beasts, savages... Eventually, it'll rip the helmet off in frustration."

There's a grunting sound, and the rocking motion stops. A flicker of dark green passes over one of the spotlights, but the creature remains out of sight.

"It came up from below," Harris says.

Jacobs' voice is scratchy over the radio. "From where I was standing just a few minutes ago?"

"Yes," Michaels says.

On the bridge of the *Dei Gratia*, no one moves. Michaels holds his breath as the creature pauses, contemplating its next move. He's expecting it to begin tearing at the suit in frustration, like a wild animal devouring a carcass.

The creature strikes the helmet, pounding the casing just above the camera. Flickers of motion flash across the screen. From what Michaels can tell, the alien's using a two-fisted strike, with both arms to concentrate its strength in much the same way a chimpanzee cracks open nuts with a rock. There are plenty of blunt objects on the floor below, plenty of things it could use as a club or a hammer. During Hubbard's exploration, Michaels saw steel trays, fire extinguishers, towel rails, chairs. Any intelligent species would look to use some kind of tool or instrument to maximize its leverage. Is this an indication of what they're dealing with, some alien creature with the strength and intelligence of an ape? Or perhaps something even more primitive, that hasn't developed even rudimentary tool skills?

One final blow destroys the camera, killing the image. Although, thinking about it, Michaels realizes it was probably a wiring fault, or a plug coming loose under the impact that caused the camera to fail, as the blows themselves weren't strong enough to crush the helmet. He wonders about the creature, curious how long it will persist in its futile attempt to crack the helmet open like an eggshell. The helmet is the toughest part of the suit and yet that's where this alien animal has focused its attention. Is this frustrated behavior indicative of low problem-solving skills?

Neither Michaels nor anyone else on the bridge hears Jacobs speaking from the icy plain below the freighter. They're mesmerized by what they've seen on the secondary screen. Michaels is still staring at the darkened monitor when Jacobs' voice snaps him back to the moment.

"... are you there? Are you reading me?"

"We read you," Vegas replies. She's shaking. Her voice no longer holds the confidence and conviction of a commander. Dr. Summers is right—they need to get off this rock.

On the main screen, Jacobs has crossed the icy plain and is opening the airlock on the scout craft. "Are you seeing this?" he asks.

There are scratches on the hull of the scout. Although the damage is superficial, it's concentrated around the airlock. Claw marks mar the sheet metal, scratching away the paint and exposing the shiny metal beneath. Michaels noted the marks were in a series of five parallel strokes roughly a foot long, consistent with what he saw on the ice, as well as the creature that tugged at Hubbard's helmet.

"This shit is freaking me out," Jacobs says.

The airlock opens, but instead of stepping inside, Jacobs turns, facing out across the plain toward the derelict star freighter. He backs inside, moving slowly. He presses the control panel on the inside of the lock and stands there watching the desolate, windswept plain as the airlock closes and seals.

"It's going to take me a few minutes to power up the scout."

"Do you want Harris to remote you in from here?" Vegas asks.

"No, I'm good," Jacobs says, his voice already sounding distant now he's removed his helmet. He turns his helmet around so they can see his face. His hair is ruffled and unkempt. His beard is damp with spittle. His eyes are wide with terror. He sets his helmet on the rack, and the microphone automatically cuts out now it's disconnected from life support and the internal battery is being recharged. Harris switches the view to an internal airlock camera on the scout, but there's no sound.

The door to the bridge of the *Dei Gratia* opens and someone walks onto the command deck. Michaels doesn't turn, neither does Vegas, or Harris. They're too engrossed in what's happening out on the frozen wasteland. Jacobs is de-suiting, removing his gloves. He's mumbling something to himself. His hands are shaking.

"Johnson's awake," a familiar voice says.

Dr. Summers drops her coffee. The plastic cup bounces as it hits the floor of the cockpit, spraying coffee across the deck. Hot coffee strikes Michaels' leg, soaking through his trousers. He turns to face Summers as the voice speaks again.

"I thought we were keeping him sedated?"

Standing there in the open hatchway of the *Dei Gratia* is First Mechanic James Stephen Hubbard III.

"What?" Hubbard asks. His hands out in front of him to

accentuate his surprise at the look he's getting from the rest of the crew. "I thought you'd want to know. It's all anyone's talking about in the Cage."

Michaels backs away from Hubbard, as does Dr. Summers.

"H—Hubbard?" Harris asks. "Is it—Is it really you?"

Hubbard seems perplexed by the question, as though he isn't sure how to respond.

"Ah, yeah," he replies with a hint of uncertainty in his voice. From Michaels' perspective, Hubbard appears genuinely surprised by the reactions he's seeing among the senior officers. "Who else would it be?"

Michaels feels his heart racing, pounding inside his chest. His hands are cold and clammy. His fingers tremble as he steps slowly backwards, feeling for the edge of the navigation desk.

Vegas turns her head slightly to one side as she steps forward toward Hubbard. Her feet glide silently across the floor as she approaches him. Cautiously, she reaches out to him.

"What the hell is wrong with you guys?" Hubbard asks. "You look like you've seen a ghost."

Vegas holds out her hand. Her fingers touch gingerly at the air between her and Hubbard, reacting as though they're touching at a force field. She moves in slow motion, the way an animal tamer might approach an upset lion, trying to soothe the creature.

Hubbard raises his eyebrows.

"Does someone want to tell me what's going on?"

On the screen behind them, Jacobs is talking, oblivious to what's going on upon the bridge of the *Dei Gratia*. He's seated in the cockpit of the tiny scout, and has a flight helmet on.

"Warming the engines... Storm's lifting, should have a smooth flight back... I've swept the inside of the ship, and rotated the external cams through 360 degrees, no sign of those things."

"Roger," Vegas replies softly, speaking into her headset. Her fingers frozen just inches from the stubble on Hubbard's chin.

"OK, this is getting really weird," Hubbard says with a sigh that sounds like one of exasperation. "What has gotten into you guys? Why is Jacobs out there alone?"

Vegas can't help herself. She has to touch him—to see if he's real.

Michaels is terrified to see Hubbard standing there on the bridge, but somehow Vegas is fearless. She reaches out and touches Hubbard's cheek as he moves slightly to one side, watching her hand closely, seemingly wondering if she's going to slap him.

"You guys are nuts," Hubbard says. Vegas pulls her hand away slowly. "Doesn't anyone care that Johnson's awake? The poor bastard is in agony."

"Ah, yeah," Dr. Summers says. She gets to her feet, ignoring the spilt coffee on the floor, and walks toward the door, edging around Hubbard. She keeps her eyes on him. Hubbard watches her with bewilderment.

"I don't know what you guys have been doing up here," Hubbard says, "but, seriously, you need to lay off the Quaaludes."

Hubbard turns to follow Dr. Summers.

"Go with them," Vegas says, addressing Michaels.

"Me?"

"You're the science officer," Vegas replies. "Do something scientific. Tell me what the hell we're dealing with here. I've got to launch a relay. We can't wait for the next orbit. The *Argo* needs to know what we're going through down here."

"Fuck me," Michaels grumbles under his breath.

"Hey, Michaels," Harris calls out after him. Michaels turns as Harris adds, "Watch your back. Take nothing for granted."

"You too."

"Oh, and Michaels," Vegas adds. "Don't let Hubbard out of your sight."

"Roger that."

Dr. Summers hurries down the hallway with Hubbard walking a few feet behind her. She keeps glancing back at him. She needs to be careful. A fall in 1.4g will hurt. It's easy to lose the center of gravity, and even a fall of a few feet can be painful. Land the wrong way, and she'll sprain something. Summers drilled the down-team before they descended to the planet's surface. If you trip and fall you're supposed to roll, and not try to break your fall. Put your hand out and you'll snap your wrist, she told them. Take your time, don't rush, that's the mantra. It's good advice, advice Summers has forgotten. She's not rushing to get to medical so much as to stay ahead of Hubbard.

Johnson is writhing in pain, calling out in agony from further down the corridor.

Dr. Summers stops in the entrance to the medical bay, staring straight ahead as though she's seen something alien.

Hubbard comes up beside her, but he looks relaxed.

Michaels catches up to them. Staring into the medical bay, he sees a row of high-set beds lining the far wall. The beds are basic, with thin foam mattresses set on a metal frame. Above them, medi-monitors line the wall. Curtains hang between the beds, drawn back and tied off. Johnson lies at the far end of the room. He's been restrained. Straps run across his chest, waist and legs, but the straps aren't tight, allowing him to twist and squirm between them. He's in danger of toppling the bed.

Michaels runs in, grabbing the end of the bed and steadying the metal frame. Johnson's eyes are wide with terror.

"They're here," he cries. "They're on the *Dei Gratia*. They're all around us."

"Who's around us?" Michaels asks, trying to calm him, holding one hand out as a gesture to hold still.

"They're everywhere."

"Who's everywhere?"

"The little green men."

Johnson reaches out from beneath one of the straps. His hand clutches at the air, wanting to touch Michaels, grabbing at him in desperation.

"Please," he says. "You've got to get me out of here."

"Doc?" Michaels says, turning toward Summers. She's still standing in the doorway, lost in a daze. Hubbard's gone. Michaels runs over and grabs Dr. Summers by the shoulders, saying, "Doc, look at me. Look into my eyes."

"Don't leave me," Johnson yells from behind him.

Dr. Summers trembles. Her pupils are dilated. Michaels feels conflicted. He doesn't know who to tend to, but he figures if Johnson can shout, he's probably in a better state than Summers at this point.

"Don't you leave me," Johnson continues to call out as he grimaces in pain, fighting against the restraints.

"Doc, I need your help here," Michaels says. "Please."

He glances both ways, looking for Hubbard in the corridor, but he's gone.

"They were here," Dr. Summers says. "I know they were. They've moved things. The curtains. The medical kits."

She feels weak in his hands, as though she's on the verge of fainting.

"Listen to me, Doc. You're in shock."

As a field medic, Michaels knows the high gravity doesn't help, making her heart fight harder to circulate blood to her head, and lowering her overall blood pressure.

"Come with me," he says, leading her inside the medical bay. He walks her over to a chair across from Johnson.

Johnson cranes his neck to see what's going on. Tubes and wires lead from his wounded shoulder—an electrical monstrosity pulsating where once there was an arm.

"Did you see them? Did you see the little green men?"

Michaels isn't sure what the appropriate response is to Johnson's question, but he figures for now it's best to humor him.

"Yes. I saw them."

"They're real," Johnson insists. He's distracting himself with his manic state. "Ha. I told you they were real. Even out there, on the ice, I knew. You laughed. You thought I was crazy, but I'm not, am I?"

"No, you're not," Michaels replies. He wraps a blanket around Dr. Summers, covering her shoulders and pulling the blanket in front of her so she can hold it closed in her lap. He touches her forehead. She feels cold, clammy.

Crouching in front of her, he asks, "What's your name?"

For a second, Summers stares through him as Johnson continues to laugh, crying out, "They're real. I told you they're real!"

"Come on, Doc. What's your name?"

Something registers deep in her eyes.

"Susan... Susan Rachel Summers."

Michaels is aware Johnson's wriggling on the bed behind him. He ignores his groans and feverish cries, forcing a fake smile as he looks Dr. Summers in the eyes.

"What day is it? Do you remember the date?"

Summers replies without missing a beat. "Sunday, December 7th, twenty-two-forty-one."

"Yeah, that's it, Doc. Twenty-third century. Now, what happened on this day? What famous event happened in history on December 7th?"

Her head turns sideways. Michaels feels as though he can see the mechanics of her mind churning as she recalls a dim memory.

"Pearl Harbor."

"That's right," Michaels says, nodding and smiling. "Three hundred years ago today. Three hundred years and a hundred and forty trillion miles away."

He points to the far wall, adding, "In that direction, if I'm not mistaken." He doesn't really know for sure. It's a guess. He's being playful, trying to engage with her.

Dr. Summers breathes deeply.

"We're a long way from home, Doc."

"Yes, we are."

"I need you, Doc. Johnson needs you."

Dr. Summers nods. Her gaze drops to the floor.

Michaels starts to stand up when Summers lashes out, grabbing his wrist.

"Please," she pleads. "Don't go. Don't leave me."

He rests his hand on hers, saying, "We're all afraid, Doc. I'm just as afraid of what's happening as you are, but I've got to find Hubbard. I've got to ask him about what happened back on the *Céleste*. I need to know how he got back here."

"He's a ghost," Summers eyes are wide.

"I'm a man of science, Doc. I don't believe in ghosts. Hubbard looks pretty damn real to me."

"But you don't know," she accuses, squeezing his wrist. "You don't know what he is."

"No, I don't," Michaels replies. "Don't you think it would be good to find out?"

Summers releases her grip.

"You're going to be fine," he says. "Everything's going to be okay. I'll get Vegas to send someone to stay with you."

Michaels turns and looks at Johnson. He's stopped thrashing around. Blankets lie on the floor. His bare legs are still. If it wasn't for the blip on the medi-monitor above his head, Michaels would have thought he was dead. His eyes are open, staring at the ceiling. Saliva dribbles from his lips. His one good arm hangs limp to the side, resting on the bed restraints.

Dr. Summers shivers. Michaels activates a computer panel on the bulkhead, putting a call through to the bridge.

"Vegas," is the terse, short reply from the other end.

"We've lost Hubbard."

"WHAT? What the hell is going on down there? Where has he gone?"

"I don't know," Michaels says. "Can you get someone down here to stay with Summers? She's not coping."

"Where are the nurses?" Vegas barks.

"I don't know, but Hubbard's gone. I need someone to take over here."

In the background, Michaels can hear Vegas talking to Harris, arranging for one of the engineers to head to the medical bay.

"Find him," she growls at Michaels, cutting the transmission.

MEMORIES

The *Dei Gratia* is three hundred meters in length, carrying four scout craft in her belly. The orbital shuttle's a heavy lifter, capable of carrying twenty times her unladen weight under a standard gravity. She looks ungainly. Her three floors are dwarfed by eight spherical tanks lined up beneath her, designed to process and store tritium for use in the *Argo's* ion-fusion drive. The *Dei Gratia* uses graviton repulsion for flight, which Vegas complains gives the ship the handling characteristics of a brick.

Michaels begins his search on the lower flight deck, above the hangar. He walks into the control booth as the outer doors close behind an incoming scout. Jacobs is back. The hangar door seals and an atmospheric purge begins, pressurizing the lock. Jets of high-pressure steam wash over the craft, melting the ice and cleaning away contaminants. The ambient light in the vast deck switches from red to green once the computer system confirms the decontamination process is complete.

Jacobs climbs out of the scout. Michaels waits for him on the other side of the inner lock. The circular door opens and Jacobs steps inside the *Dei Gratia* looking weary from more than the gravity. His shoulders are stooped, his eyes bloodshot. His hair is matted down with sweat.

"We need to talk."

Jacobs barely acknowledges him. He hangs his flight helmet on the rack and sits down to take off his boots. Through the thick glass window in the lock, Michaels can see one of the flight engineers already refueling the scout.

"We need to get off this fucking planet," Jacobs says, sounding exasperated.

"The *Argo* needs that tritium."

"At what price?" Jacobs asks. "This was supposed to be a straightforward mining drop. No more than three days of surface ops."

Michaels nods.

"I need to talk to you about Hubbard."

Jacobs looks up at him. His body seems to stiffen.

Michaels isn't sure where to begin, or quite how to explain what's happened.

"He's here... somewhere."

"What?" Jacobs' eyes narrow. His head cocks slightly to one side as he sits there facing Michaels. "What the hell are you talking about?"

"He walked onto the bridge." Michaels says, although his words sound dumb. He's flustered, unsure quite how to explain what's transpired. His comment certainly isn't an explanation.

"Are you fucking mad?" Jacobs cries, gesturing with his arm toward the airlock. "He died out there! I saw him. I held his *fucking* hand."

"I know."

Jacobs spits on the floor.

Michaels is surprised by how hard it is to formulate any kind of plausible explanation for what's transpired. "Hubbard doesn't know what happened, at least not as far as I can tell."

"Is this some kind of sick joke?" Jacobs asks.

Michaels feels his upper lip pull taut with emotion as he struggles to say, "No. I wish it was."

Jacobs wriggles out of his inner thermal suit and clips it on the rack.

"Where is he?" the weary astronaut asks.

"I was hoping you might know," Michaels replies. "You knew him better than anyone else."

"I hated him more than anyone else."

Jacobs scratches his head, adding, "Ah, shit. Look, I don't know what the hell is going on here. Hubbard's dead, OK? His body is freezing into a popsicle somewhere over a hundred clicks west of here. There's no way he's on the *Dei Gratia*."

"If he was," Michaels asks. "Where would he go?"

Jacobs thinks for a second, replying, "Back on the *Argo*, he'd spend time in the gym, or the nest. For all his bluster, he was a bit of a loner, didn't like crowds."

"Thanks," Michaels says, nodding as he gets to his feet.

"What the hell is going on, Michaels?"

"I don't know."

There's no gym on the *Dei Gratia*, but the shuttle has a crow's nest located in the stern of the ship at the base of the tail fin. The crow's nest is redundant on a mining shuttle, used only as a maintenance airlock to gain access to the aft portion of the craft.

Michaels stops in the ready room and places a call to Vegas.

"Jacobs is back."

"How did he take it?" Vegas asks.

"He thinks we're full of shit," Michaels answers.

"He's right," Vegas says, and from the tone of her voice Michaels figures she's not being sarcastic. She agrees.

"Jacobs thinks Hubbard may be in the crow's nest. Apparently, he heads up there from time to time."

"OK, check it out," Vegas says. "Oh, and grab a disruptor. If you run into trouble, kill him. Is that understood?"

Michaels swallows the knot in his throat as he forces out, "Yes."

"Don't hesitate. Don't second guess yourself. Kill him," Vegas repeats.

Michaels nods, not that Vegas would know it. A soft crackle in the speaker stops and Michaels knows she's cut the transmission. He opens one of the mining lockers and rummages through the equipment until he comes across a mineral disruptor. The disruptors use subatomic pulses to fragment rocks. When used on a person, the results are messy at best.

Michaels puts the disrupter in his jacket pocket and runs the length of the ship, using his arms to steady himself on the walls, grabbing hold of the railing to stop himself from falling awkwardly in the oppressive gravity. Crewmembers watch in surprise as he races by. They stay out of his way. By the end of the corridor, Michaels has covered what is the equivalent of a stair climb through 15-20 stories on Earth, only he's travelled in a straight line on this planet. His feet feel like lead weights. His calf muscles ache. His knees are sore. His lungs scream for oxygen. He stops to catch his breath.

The rear of the *Dei Gratia* is a maze of ducts and pipes, and Michaels is all too aware anything could be hiding back here. The engines are idling, keeping electricity running throughout the ship and preventing the craft from icing up in the extreme cold. The hum resonates through the steel grating on the suspended floor in engineering. Mechanics ignore him, conducting maintenance on the coils and injector rods surrounding the main engine. The engine housing glows in a warm red. Even from where he is almost thirty feet away, he can feel the radiant heat. They must have the internal baffles open and the magnetic shielding down, allowing heat to dissipate throughout the ship.

Sweat drips from his forehead.

Michaels walks on with his hands on his hips, sucking in air. Ahead, he can see the rear bulkhead. A ladder leads to the tail section.

He climbs carefully, aware his palms are sweaty, making the ladder rungs slippery.

The duct twists on an angle, following the gradient of the tail fin housing the cooling pumps. The duct opens out into a small landing containing an airlock. The ladder continues on another fifteen feet and finishes at the observation deck. Michaels takes his time, being careful to observe the details around him, not wanting to miss something important. Two suits hang on the rack. Dust lines the floor. Nothing looks out of place. He continues on.

Above, a lone figure sits in the darkness, staring out through the floor-to-ceiling windows. Michaels climbs the last few rungs slowly, not sure if Hubbard is aware he's there. Sudden moves don't seem like a good idea.

Outside, the storm lashes the windows. The flashing of a navigation light above the bridge is visible through the sleet. Darkness has fallen. Technically, it's still morning on the *Argo*, but the planet has a rotation of 27 hours, making the days uncomfortably long. Lightning ripples through the clouds. Under any other circumstance, Michaels would enjoy sitting there staring out at the electrical storm, in awe of its raw power.

"Hey," he says softly, stepping from the rails to the floor.

Hubbard turns toward him but doesn't say anything. In the darkness, Michaels can't make out more than a silhouette. Every few seconds, a flash of lightning illuminates the observation deck, giving Hubbard's drawn features a haggard, ominous look.

"Can we talk?"

"Sure," Hubbard replies, gesturing to the bench seat beside him.

Michaels breathes deeply, his nerves on edge.

"What happened out there? What do you remember?"

"I don't know what you mean," Hubbard says.

"You know what I'm talking about," Michaels says, "But I want to hear it from you—in your words. What happened during the EVA?"

"EVA?" Hubbard asks with a semblance of surprise. "You were the one on EVA, Michaels. You and Johnson. What about you tell me what happened during your EVA by the thermal pools? Why don't you come clean about what's really out there? You tell me why has Vegas removed both the video feed and the log files of your EVA from the core?"

Michaels ignores him. "This isn't about me. Tell me what you saw."

Hubbard turns to him, grinning as he says, "What are you? A shrink? I thought psychoanalysis was the purview of Doc Summers."

"Summers isn't doing so well," Michaels says, trying to hide his trembling hands. "This planet has her spooked."

Hubbard grunts in agreement. "She's not the only one."

Michaels isn't getting anywhere with Hubbard, if this really is Hubbard. Michaels has to change tack. Lightning ripples through the clouds rolling above them. Wind buffets the tail section of the craft, causing the superstructure to creak and groan.

"Magnificent, isn't it?" Hubbard asks, looking out at the raging storm.

"Sure is," Michaels says, but he's more interested in the tablet computer in Hubbard's hands. "What are you reading?"

"History."

"History?" Michaels replies, genuinely surprised.

"History," Hubbard says a second time, but he doesn't elaborate on that one word.

"Do you mind?" Michaels asks, reaching for the tablet.

"Sure," Hubbard says, handing the computer to him. "We have nothing but history to hold to. There is no future, only history repeating itself time and again. Names change, dates advance, but history is always the same."

Michaels ignores his cryptic comment and swipes his hand, opening the device.

Captain James Cook

Journal of Proceedings from the Voyage of H.M. Endeavour

1768-1771

The tablet opens at the first page of an ancient historical document, but there's a bookmark. Michaels presses the mark and a highlighted entry appears on the screen. He wants to read it, but he can't focus his mind on the words. His eyes skim across the electronic page, taking in only the salient points, and he finds himself missing most of the content. It's the tension of the moment, but this is important. He feels he has to pay attention to the subtleties surrounding Hubbard if he's going to unravel this mystery. Michaels breathes deeply, calming himself. He forces himself to slow down and read with awareness, resisting the temptation to gloss over the finer details.

Botany Bay, Australia:

We stood into the bay and anchored under the south shore about two miles within the entrance in five fathoms... Saw, as we came in, on both points of the bay, several of the Natives and a few huts; men, women, and children on the south shore abreast of our ship, to which place I went in the boats in hopes of speaking with them, accompanied by Mr. Banks, Dr. Solander, and Tupia.

As we approached the Shore they all made off, except two men, who seem'd resolved to oppose our landing. As soon as I saw this I order'd the boats to lay upon their Oars, in order to speak to them; but this was to little purpose, for neither us nor Tupia could understand one word they said. We then threw them some nails, beads, etc., a shore, which they took up, and seem'd not ill pleased with, in so much that I thought that they beckon'd to us to come ashore; but in this we were mistaken, for as soon as we put the boat in they again came to oppose us, upon which I fir'd a musket between the two, which had no other effect than to make them retire back where bundles of their darts lay, and one of them took up a stone and threw at us, which caused my firing a second musket, loaded with small shot; and altho' some of the shot struck the man, yet it had no other effect than making him lay hold on a target. Immediately after this we landed, which we had no sooner done than they throw'd two darts at us; this obliged me to fire a third shot, soon after which they both made off...

"What is this?" Michaels asks, not understanding why Hubbard would highlight these words.

"What does it look like?" Hubbard asks in reply. "First Contact."

Michaels nods, surprised by his response.

"And you think that's what's happening here?"

"Yes," Hubbard replies. "You disagree?"

"No."

Michaels is flabbergasted. He isn't sure quite what he expected when he caught up with Hubbard. Some deep, dark fear suggested hostility, but he dismissed that as nothing more than primitive superstition—fight or flight—the fear of a monster under the bed—and yet Hubbard is dead. Michaels watched Hubbard die. He watched as an alien creature fought to remove his helmet. This can't be Hubbard, not as Michaels once knew him, and if this isn't Hubbard, who the hell is it? And why is it reading up on the ancient exploration of Earth?

"Tell me about the bridge of the *Céleste*," Michaels says in a matter-of-fact tone. His Hubbard never made it to the bridge of the *Céleste*, has this one made it that far?

"The *Céleste*?" Hubbard is surprised. "I've never set foot on the *Céleste*."

Michaels bites his lip, he's getting nowhere.

"We need to get you checked out," he says, not sure what he's dealing with, but wondering if a medical scan might reveal something untoward. His mind runs to a number of different possible scenarios, including the possibility of parallel universes colliding, or conflicting timelines merging, but none of these make any sense. At best, they're theoretical concepts. At worst, fantasy.

"By Doc?"

"Yeah. You may have been exposed to something."

"That's bullshit," Hubbard snaps, becoming defensive. "What the hell's going on, Michaels?"

"What do you mean?" Michaels asks, intrigued by the dynamic at play between them—the unspoken agreement not to talk about what really happened on board the Céleste.

"I mean, I was hermetically sealed in my EVA suit during maintenance operations. I was no more exposed to anything than you were, and you waded through a *goddamn* alien thermal spring. Why don't you tell me what's really going on? What the hell happened to Johnson by the hot pools? And what the *fuck* does that have to do with me?"

Michaels runs his hands through his hair, unsure what to say next. He breathes deeply, exhaling before he says, "You died."

"What?" Hubbard almost shouts. "Do you realize how crazy you sound right now? I mean, you're sitting next to me telling me I'm dead. Have you lost your *fucking* mind? In case you haven't noticed, I'm right here, alive and breathing."

Michaels repeats himself. "I'm sorry, but you never made it back to the *Dei Gratia*. You never even made it to the bridge of the *Céleste*. You died out there."

"This is a joke. A sick fucking joke. Did Jacobs put you up to this?"

Michaels clenches his lips, unsure what to say.

Hubbard's silent.

Michaels brings up the ship's central computer on the tablet and downloads the logs from the survey. Hubbard watches in silence as the video plays before him. He hears himself talking, and sees himself walking through the darkened abandoned star freighter. Although the majority of the footage is from the perspective of his helmet camera, there are several shots from Jacobs' viewpoint, clearly catching Hubbard's face in the lights.

"It's not me," he mumbles.

A couple of times, Hubbard scrubs back and forth along the timeline, rewinding and replaying sections such as the interaction with the alien creature in the sleeping berth. Hubbard's stoic as he watches himself slip and fall in the maintenance shaft.

"That's not me," he insists even though the readout shows his name and vital signs slowly fading away. "I swear, Michaels. That is not me. You've got the wrong man."

Michaels breathes deeply and says, "I'm sorry."

"This is unreal," Hubbard says. "What has that fucker Jacobs done this time? He jumps at goddamn shadows?"

"Hey," Michaels replies. "Calm down."

"Calm down," Hubbard exclaims. "You're telling me I died on some derelict spacecraft that crashed on this godforsaken shit hole and you want me to calm down? Fuck you, Michaels. *Fuck you.*"

Hubbard springs to his feet and begins pacing back and forth. Lightning crackles through the sky behind him. Thunder shakes the craft. The storm lashes the windows, apparently trying to break through.

"Does Vegas know about this?" Hubbard asks, pointing at the computer tablet.

"She saw it in real time."

Hubbard runs his fingers through his hair, "I can't believe this. I can't believe you think this is real. What is wrong with you?"

"You don't remember any of it, do you?" Michaels asks.

"No. None of it, because it *never* happened. I was asleep in the dorm. I woke up hearing Johnson screaming and went to help."

Michaels can feel his heart racing in his chest. He tries to keep a calm demeanor, but his voice betrays him, wavering as he speaks. "What about the return flight? Do you remember how you got back to the *Dei Gratia*?"

Michaels can see Hubbard's eyes glazing over, looking into the middle distance. He's lost in thought.

"You don't remember, do you?"

"I wasn't there. I can't have been. I—"

"You're not sure, are you?"

Hubbard pauses, standing still as the storm increases in its ferocity behind him. Methane ice pummels the window, coming down in sheets, pelting the observation deck. Lightning cuts through the night—jagged streaks of blue and white slash a path through the dark clouds, splintering as they dissipate overhead. The storm has the ferocity of a caged animal, wild and clawing at the bars, desperate to break in.

Hubbard sinks to his knees. He bows his head as lightning strikes the starboard engine casing, casting a neon glow around them for the briefest of moments as the electricity dissipates.

"This can't be," Hubbard says with his hands over his face. At first, Michaels wonders if he's crying as he seems distraught, but there aren't any tears.

"What does this mean?" he asks, looking up at Michaels.

"You need to come with me."

"No," Hubbard cries as a crack of lightning bursts directly overhead. The resounding thunder shakes the *Dei Gratia*.

"You *have* to come with me," Michaels insists.

Michaels finds his fingers tightening around the disruptor in his pocket. He hopes he doesn't have to threaten Hubbard, and he wonders if he has the nerve to go through with using the disruptor if it comes to it.

Hubbard looks him in the eye. His gaze appears to see through into Michaels' very soul. Michaels is shaking. Hubbard eyes him coldly. He gestures to the ladder rungs.

"After you," Michaels says.

There's no way Michaels is going in front of Hubbard.

MEDICAL

Michaels can hear the screams before he turns into the corridor leading to the medical bay. His blood runs cold. He pulls the disruptor from his pocket and holds it by his side. Hubbard glances at the device and tightens his lips, probably because he realizes Michaels is carrying it as a last resort for use against him.

Hubbard slows to drop behind Michaels, but Michaels shakes his head and gestures with his hand, urging Hubbard on ahead.

From the corner, Michaels can see blood splattered across the floor and wall opposite the medical bay. A blood curdling howl resounds from the bay. The metallic sound of a bed crashing to the floor sets his nerves on end.

Hubbard pauses, speaking under his breath.

"There is no *fucking* way I am going in there."

Michaels flicks the power cycle on the disruptor and feels the gun hum in his hand. He nods with his head, indicating that Hubbard should continue on.

"Go ahead. Shoot me," Hubbard says, forgetting to whisper. "I am not going in there if one of those things is loose onboard. You might think I'm dead, but I'd beg to differ and, besides, if I am dead, I have no intention of a repeat performance."

"Stay out of sight," Michaels says, stepping past him.

"Where am I going to go?" Hubbard asks. "In here, out there, those damn things are everywhere."

Michaels leaves Hubbard at the corner of the corridor beside an alcove containing a fire suppression kit. He creeps forward. The screaming stops abruptly. Over the soft squeak of his shoes on the slick floor he can hear someone whimpering in the medical bay.

He doesn't like having his back to Hubbard, but he has no choice. Fear has been replaced with intrigue, and he remembers the bravado of Hubbard on the *Céleste,* talking about a feeling of compulsion to go on after he ran into the creature in the crew berth. He had to know, that was the phrase he used, and now Michaels feels the same instinctive drive. He has to see around the corner. He has to see them for himself. A fleeting glance on the ice wasn't enough to quench his curiosity. He has to examine one of these alien creatures up close. His heart thumps in his chest.

Claws reach around the doorframe, but they're directed away from him, toward the bridge. He raises his disruptor, holding it at arm's length, primed, ready to fire. The alien hasn't seen him. He can make out the side of its hairless head bobbing up and down from behind. From the sound, Michaels assumes it's licking the wall, licking at the fresh blood.

He pushes his back against the outside wall as he inches his way down the corridor, keeping himself in the creature's blind spot, with his disruptor trained on its head.

The phrase *little green men* is apt, he thinks. Although he can only see part of the creature, it's no more than four feet in height. Its naked torso is small and thin. Long spindly arms and dangly legs move in an erratic motion, as though the ungainly alien is a puppet. With fingers splayed, the creature licks at the doorjamb, standing on tiptoe to reach the splatter as it sucks at the fresh blood.

There's a crash from inside the medical bay. Someone or something has knocked over a tray, sending tweezers, sutures, and small steel pans clattering across the floor. Michaels feels his heart jump. The creature darts back into the room.

His hands tremble. His feet feel heavy and clumsy, as though at any moment they might betray him by collapsing beneath him. Michaels feels lightheaded, in much the same way he does during a launch when the blood rushes from his head to his extremities. He tightens his grip on the disruptor, watching as it shakes in his hand.

Slowly, he edges his way to the door and peers inside. Johnson is lying on the bed at the far end of the room, with Dr. Summers crouched in the corner beyond him. She's trying to make herself as small and inconspicuous as possible. She has her hand over her mouth. Given the expression on her face, it's to stop herself from crying out in terror.

Dr. Summers sees him. Their eyes lock. Her eyes widen as her brow raises, and he signals to her with his empty hand, wanting her to stay put, to keep calm and not move.

Michaels breathes deeply, thinking about his options. The

creatures haven't attacked either Summers or Johnson, but they must know they're there. Even from where he is, he can see Summers shaking. Her face is pale and gaunt.

A bed frame skids across the floor and out the door, sliding on the pool of blood seeping into the hallway before banging into the wall. The creatures, it seems, are growing more violent. How many are there? By his reckoning, there are at least two—the one he saw, and another traipsing around bumping into medical equipment, although there could be three, four or possibly five of them for all he knows. What does he think he can do? Standing there, Michaels realizes he should never have come down the corridor alone. He should have reached out to Vegas and organized a team to come at these creatures from both directions. He considers edging his way back to Hubbard, but he can see the terror in Dr. Summer's eyes. He can't abandon her.

Against his better judgment, he inches forward.

A bloodied arm lies on the floor inside the medical bay. He isn't sure if it's from a nurse or one of the miners, but he can hear the soft squelch of an animal tearing at flesh, and the crunch of bones being ground between teeth.

He knows these creatures are fast. He's seen their speed and agility on the ice. He saw the creature in the doorway spring away from the opening in a fraction of a second, and he knows if he exposes himself he'll get time for one shot, maybe two before they react and spring for cover, or charge at him.

Doubts play in his mind. How good a shot is he? Disruptors are designed to be pushed hard against a rock, not fired from a distance, even if that is only a few feet away. How accurate will his shot be? And with his arm trembling, he could easily miss. He doesn't like his chances, but he has no choice. He can't abandon Summers or Johnson.

Michaels steels himself, preparing to spring when he hears the sound of breathing behind him. His muscles tighten. Sweat beads on his brow. He dares not breathe. Slowly, he turns and catches a glimpse of one of the creatures out of the corner of his eye. The alien is not more than a foot away, it crept up behind him. Claws reach for him. Dark, beady eyes speak of raw, animal aggression, coiled and tense, desperate to be unleashed.

Physically, Michaels is still facing forward, but he's looking back over his shoulder. Another creature snarls, growling from in front of him. They're surrounding him. He freezes. Rather than fight or flight, his mind shuts down, paralyzing him with fear. His legs shake.

"Nooo!" Dr. Summers screams, and Michaels turns slowly back toward her. Bloody teeth snarl inches from his face. Yet another alien moves inside the room, knocking into metal carts and upturning chairs as it dashes out into the hallway to face him.

Michaels shudders at the prospect of being eaten alive. He only hopes death will come quick. Will shock numb him from the physical pain? Will his senses be overwhelmed, causing him to black out in those final few seconds? He knows he's going to die, he only hopes it will be mercifully quick and painless, although he doubts he'll get his wish.

Hubbard yells from somewhere behind him, surprising both him and the aliens. Michaels had forgotten about Hubbard.

Michaels turns. His feet won't move, but he twists from his hips. He can't help himself. Even though he feels it's a mistake, he can't keep his eyes on the creature in front of him. He has to see Hubbard.

Hubbard runs down the hallway toward him like a madman, running as hard and as fast as he can with a CO_2 fire extinguisher shooting white clouds of freezing cold gas out ahead of him. He waves the broad nozzle with one hand, heaving the large red cylinder with the other as he sprays the corridor with a thick white cloud of carbon dioxide.

He can't hurt these creatures. He must know that. If they can survive in the noxious atmosphere of this frozen planet, a burst of CO_2 won't harm them. Hubbard is trying to upset them, to disorient and scare them. He's yelling, screaming as he runs in with the extinguisher billowing white vapor, blanketing the corridor in a waist-deep fog. It's bluster, a bluff, a hollow, meaningless threat.

Michaels screams as well, yelling with all his might and projecting his voice from his diaphragm, roaring like a lion on the savannah.

White gas billows around them. The two men push their backs against each other, turning as they yell. Hubbard continues to fire the extinguisher, blanketing the corridor. In the white haze, Michaels loses sight of the creatures, but he's alive—they haven't torn him to shreds.

After a few seconds, Hubbard eases up on the trigger, and their yelling fades like the mist around them. The gas dissipates. The creatures are gone.

Johnson mumbles. He's still strapped to the bed at the far end of the medical bay, but he's talking under his breath, speaking rapidly—Michaels can't make out the words.

Summers hasn't moved.

Michaels staggers against the far wall, facing the open medi-bay doors. His legs buckle beneath him. He's shaking violently. The disruptor lies on the ground. He can't remember dropping it, but he has. He slides down the wall and slumps onto the bloodstained floor.

Hubbard drops the fire extinguisher, allowing it to fall against the floor. He too is shaking. He looks down at his trembling hands. Slowly, he slides to the floor opposite Michaels.

"Well," he says. "That worked better than I expected."

"How—How did you know?" Michaels asks, looking at the extinguisher lying on the floor between them.

"I didn't."

"Then why? Why risk your life?"

"Because I'm already dead, remember?" Hubbard answers.

Michaels smiles, saying, "Thank you."

Further down the corridor, Vegas and Harris run toward them. They're carrying large mining lasers in both hands, holding them like rifles. Several other miners run in support of them.

There are bloody footprints scattered across the floor. They lead away from the two men, back toward engineering.

"I can't do this," Michaels confided in Hubbard. "I can't go on like this."

He looks over at Summers. She's catatonic. She rocks back and forth, mumbling to herself like Johnson.

"I'll end up like them."

Hubbard turns and looks at Summers. His lips tighten. The lines on his face look like scars.

"There has to be a reason for what's happening," Hubbard says. "There's got to be answers."

"No," Michaels replies, disagreeing. "No, there doesn't. Reality is chaotic. There's no rhyme or reason to carnage. Sometimes in life there are no answers, and so any answers we come up with are little more than wishful thinking. These beasts, these monsters, they know not reason. They're not intelligent like us. They're primitive, base and brute. You can no more reason with them than you can reason with a fire."

Michaels feels lost. His head hangs low.

FIRE

"How the hell did they get on board?" Vegas asks, pacing on the bridge of the *Dei Gratia*.

The bulk of the crew has gathered in the hangar, ready for evac, but Vegas has kept the command group together on the bridge, she isn't willing to give up her ship without a fight. Summers and Johnson are already strapped into one of the scouts, ready to launch. Michaels wanted to go with them, but Vegas insisted on his help.

Jacobs warms his hand against a cup of coffee, like Summers before him, he's hiding his trembling hands.

"I've checked the logs," Harris replies. "We've had no unauthorized access through any of the airlocks."

Vegas asks, "Is there any other way they could get in?"

"No. Any hull breach would result in a pressure differential that would cause the affected compartment to be automatically sealed."

"Could they have breached the hull without causing a loss of pressure?" Vegas asks, turning to Michaels.

"Unknown," is all he can bring himself to say.

Harris hands him a cup of coffee. Michaels struggles to take the drink without spilling it. Even with a concerted effort, his hands continue to shake.

"What do you mean, unknown?" Vegas asks. "Unknown is a single word, not a sentence, not an explanation. You're the *goddamn* science officer, give me some scientific reason behind all this, not a grunt in response."

Michaels breathes deeply, trying not to let Vegas provoke him. She's under pressure. They all are.

"Without learning more about these creatures, there's no way to know whether they could have breached the hull without causing at least some change in both pressure and atmospheric mix. In theory, they could have some means we're not aware of, but in practice, I think that would be highly unlikely, and yet they're here. How they pulled this off is unknown, and by unknown I mean, not readily apparent. If you want to get to the bottom of how, I'd need to survey the hull from the outside to find their point of entry. That would take hours."

Vegas paces the floor. She doesn't respond. Whether his answer satisfied her or not is difficult to ascertain. Michaels figures she doesn't like his response, but at that moment she wouldn't like any response short of an absolute answer.

"We need to abandon ship," Jacobs says. "Cut our losses and get out of here while we still can."

"We are *not*," Vegas says with strident passion, "abandoning a twenty-seven trillion dollar exploration vehicle because you've lost your nerve."

"You saw what those things did," Jacobs protests. "They'll kill us all."

Vegas ignores him.

"Can we track them?" she asks, turning to Harris.

"Only on the upper corridors. There are a few cameras on the lower deck, and down in engineering, but not enough to give us good coverage. If they get in the ducts, they'll be practically invisible."

"Can we flush them out?" Vegas asks Michaels. "Blow the locks?"

Michaels raises his eyebrows at the thought.

"I'm not sure that would do any good," he replies. "This is their world. And the pressure difference is against us. We'd push them further in rather than blow them out, and we'd have to decontaminate the ship before we could use her again."

"What about from orbit?" she asks. "Using vacuum?"

Michaels sips his coffee. His hands have stopped shaking. Engaging his mind is good for his nerves.

"Rapid depressurization is not a good idea. We'd lose a lot of good air, and it would only clear out areas immediately around the lock. It could cause significant damage to the ship."

"How long do you think they could hold their breath?" Harris asks.

"I don't even know that they breathe," Michaels says. "They probably have some equivalent of respiration, but I don't know how they'd respond at a biological level. We can only survive without oxygen for seconds to minutes, but whales can survive for hours. There are spiders that can hold their breath underwater for days. Then there are creatures like tardigrades that can survive almost indefinitely in a frozen vacuum, only to wake when conditions return to favorable. We have no idea what the effect of a vacuum would be on these creatures, and no reason to think such a tactic would work."

Vegas nods, but her motion is begrudging, as though she's fighting her own frustrations.

A voice speaks from the shadows.

"Clear them out room by room." Hubbard steps forward as he says, "We do this the old fashioned way, like island hopping during World War II in the Pacific."

"You're not seriously going to–" Jacobs begins, but Vegas cuts him off.

"Go on."

"These things are afraid of fire, right?" Hubbard asks, turning toward Michaels. "So we use that fear against them."

"Could work," Michaels replies. "Light and heat. Every time we've run into them, it's been the introduction of large quantities of light or heat that have warned them off. On the ice, they stayed out of our spotlights, attacking from behind. Once I lit the flare, they kept their distance. The same principle held on the *Céleste*."

"What about in the medical bay?" Harris asks.

"I don't think it was the CO_2 that scared them, it was the brilliant white clouds, the glare, the sudden shift in albedo."

"Maybe they're nocturnal," Hubbard says.

"I'm not sure, but like any animal, rapid change is frightening, and elicits a flight response. We could use that to our advantage."

"So we burn them out?" Vegas asks.

Michaels says, "Given their natural environment is a frozen wasteland, I suspect fire would be particularly effective."

"Wait a minute," Jacobs says, pointing at Hubbard. "All this stemmed from Hubbard's comment. You're not going to take advice from that... that thing?"

Michaels interjects, saying, "*That thing*, as you so aptly put it, saved my life. He could have died along with me."

"Hey–" Vegas says, but this time Jacobs cuts her off.

"Not he. It! Hubbard died on the *Céleste*, remember? I don't know what that thing is, but they sent it here to mislead us, to deceive us, and you've been taken in by it! All of you. You think the monsters are out there? You think those little green men are all you've got to worry about? What about this Trojan Horse? Hubbard's the real monster."

"Shut your mouth," Hubbard snaps.

"Or what?" Jacobs asks. "Are you going to disembowel me like one of them? Or is some goddamn alien about to burst out of your chest?"

Hubbard lunges at Jacobs, grabbing him by the throat.

Jacobs twists to one side, lashing out at Hubbard. He lands a punch on his face, catching Hubbard square on his nose. Blood sprays on both sides of his face.

Hubbard strikes Jacobs on the jaw. Neither man pulls his punches. Each blow lands with a staggering amount of force, with both men going for headshots. There is no consideration given to defense. They trade punches with relentless ferocity, pounding each other. Bloodied fists fly through the air.

"STOP THIS MADNESS," Vegas screams as the two men slug at each other. There's no doubt in Michaels' mind that the only way this fight will end is with someone's death. Harris grabs Jacobs by the shoulders, pulling him away, while Michaels struggles to restrain Hubbard, wrestling him away from Jacobs. Still blows land, striking jaws and cheekbones. Jacobs takes a cut above his right eye, while Hubbard has a stream of blood running down his face, staining his white shirt bright red.

The power goes off. The bridge is plunged into darkness, and the bulkhead automatically seals, closing them in on the bridge. The fighting stops as fear descends.

A crackle of lightning flashes through the windows at the front of the craft. The darkened consoles and chairs cast long shadows throughout the bridge.

The change in dynamic causes the two men to stop fighting. They stand there stunned as the emergency lighting comes on, soaking the bridge in a blood-red hue.

"Fuck!" Harris cries. "They've cut the power."

"I thought you said they weren't intelligent?" Vegas asks, turning to Michaels.

"They seem pretty damn smart to me," Harris says.

Michaels doesn't know what to say in response. Hubbard relaxes so Michaels lets him go. Harris brings up a single white light directly overhead.

"What's the damage?" Vegas asks.

Harris is already at a console, powering it up into text-only mode, and pulling up log files.

"Well," he says. "We're not going anywhere fast. For now, only the core systems are online. The bridge has its own reserves of power and air, designed to last twenty-four hours in space. Down here, with convective heat loss, we'll burn through our electrical power in five, maybe six hours."

"What about the hangar?"

"They can use emergency power to cycle the lock and open the outer doors, but only as long as their local emergency power supply lasts. After that, they're stuck."

"OK, get them out of there," Vegas commands.

Harris passes on the order as Jacobs protests, "What about us? We could make it to the hangar!"

"We're not abandoning the *Dei Gratia*," Vegas snaps. "They've got the *Céleste*. I'm not leaving another ship to freeze on the ice. We'll wait for the *Argo* to effect a rescue during the next orbit."

"Shit!" Jacobs swears.

Harris says, "We're going to need to get that power back on soon or this place is going to turn into a freezer."

"Son of a..." Jacobs yells, pounding his fist on a sheet metal locker. He strikes the panel several times in succession. In the deafening silence that follows his tantrum, a distant knocking echoes in reply. Michaels feels his blood run cold.

Harris starts to say something but Michaels holds out his hand, saying, "Shush." He leans forward as he approaches the door. The faint sound of scratching can be heard, followed by a fist banging in mimicry of Jacobs.

"We're fucked," Jacobs says. "We are so fucked."

"No disagreement here," Hubbard replies, wiping the blood from his nose on the back of his forearm.

"I've isolated the problem," Harris says. "There's a junction box in engineering channeling primary power from the core. Something's shorted the breakers. If I can get down there, I can fix this. All it needs is a hardwire across the junction to force the connection."

"You want to go out there?" Jacobs blurts in amazement, pointing at the sealed door. "No, I say we sit tight and wait for the *Argo*."

"We'll be popsicles inside a day," Harris replies.

Michaels feels he understands the practicalities of the situation. He says, "It's going to take the *Argo* time to prep a rescue ship. With transit time, and allowing for repairs, not to mention any hostilities with our friends, any rescue is probably eight to twelve hours away, at least."

Jacobs is quiet. Michaels can see him simmering, still brooding over the fight with Hubbard.

"What did you salvage from the stores?" Vegas asks Harris.

"Two mining lasers, a propane torch, and three disruptors."

Harris uses two hands to haul a large gas tank up onto the navigation desk.

"The propane's our best option. The disruptors are only good at close quarters, you've got to push them hard against an object to have any real effect. The mining lasers could work, but if we power them up to full strength a miss would risk a hull breach. At low power, they need to be held on target for a few seconds before they penetrate to any depth, and I doubt these guys are going to oblige by standing still."

"But the propane torch?" Michaels asks.

"It's not designed to run directly from the tank, but I can bypass the valve and use a direct feed. Pressure should be good from the tank. If I crimp the outlet, we should have enough pressure to get about twenty to thirty feet of flame."

"But?" Michaels asks. From the look on Harris' face he figures there's a catch.

"But this thing was designed for brazing and soldering. If we're not careful, we'll overheat the damned thing. The trick is going to be to move the ignition circuit."

Harris is already tinkering with the torch, unscrewing a module on the side.

"With the propane coming out in a thin stream under pressure, we'll be able to get a good oxygen mix in the air and hit some seriously high temperatures."

"Such as?" Vegas asks.

"With the air intake fully open, fifteen hundred, maybe two thousand degrees."

Jacobs has his hand raised, wanting to ask a question. "Does it strike anyone else as a really bad idea to burn down our own spaceship?"

Hubbard smiles. No one else seems to think he's funny.

"Most of the material onboard is flame retardant," Michaels says. "The real problem is going to be toxic fumes coming off whatever *does* burn. You're going to need a suit or a mask, or you're not going to make it to the end of the floor."

"We'll be able to get breathing apparatus at one of the emergency stations," Harris replies. "There's one at the end of the corridor."

"What about the ship's fire suppression system?" Vegas asks.

"Without power, only the failsafe systems are operational," Harris says. "There are thermal heads at the major junctions. If we light up one of those there's going to be torrential rain."

"Can we deactivate the system?" Michaels asks.

"No," Harris says. "It's mechanical by design, as in failing-on. In zero-gee, it comes out as a fine spray and is sucked up by a vacuum pump, but in a gravity well like this it has to run off. I guess the architects never counted on anyone hunting down murderous aliens with a flamethrower."

"Guess not," Vegas says, agreeing with him.

Harris lights the pilot light and both Hubbard and Michaels move out of the way. He opens up the feed line and gives it a short burst. A ball of fire rolls through the air. Black smoke curls up toward the ceiling as a wave of heat washes over them.

"That'll work," Harris says with a grin.

"I want to go," Michaels says, blurting out those four words with a hint of resignation in his voice. He feels responsible. He and Johnson first stirred these creatures by the thermal pool. If anyone's going to risk their lives, he ought to be among them.

"You don't have to do this," Harris replies. "I'm the only one who can fix that junction box."

"That's exactly my point," Michaels says. "You're going to need someone to drag this propane tank around, someone to cover you while you work on the box, someone to help out if you run into these creatures."

"I need you here with me," Vegas says to Michaels. "We've got to figure out what the hell these things are."

"I'll go," Hubbard says softly.

"I don't know what use I'll be to you here," Michaels says, replying to Vegas and missing Hubbard's comment.

"Take me."

"Hell, yes," Jacobs says, pointing. "Send Hubbard."

Harris nods, agreeing with the idea. Vegas doesn't look impressed by Jacobs.

"You can go too," she says.

"Me? Hell no."

"Hell, yes," Vegas says. "You're dead weight here. The three of you will need to work together, but you can make it."

"Goddamn it," Jacobs complains.

Hubbard slaps him on the back and smiles, saying, "What are you afraid of? What could possibly go wrong?"

Jacobs is not impressed with Hubbard goading him. "What if I don't go? You can't make me."

Vegas steps up to Jacobs, going toe-to-toe with him and invading his personal space as she backs him up against the bulkhead. "Listen here, Jacobs. This isn't a *fucking* game. This isn't one of your pissing contests where you can mouth off and play the fool. You will do as you're commanded. And why? Because it's the right thing to do—because I will not let you shrink in fear—because our lives depend on you guys getting to that junction box and bringing the *Dei Gratia* back online. Is that understood?"

No one breathes.

Jacobs nods, his eyes cast down at the ground. Jacobs must feel as though he is being press-ganged into service, but the reality is they have no choice. Whether they go for engineering or the hangar, they have to brave the darkness.

Harris breaks the silence, saying, "We've got dozens of penlights. They provide focused light when repairing a circuit board. They won't throw out much ambient light, but they'll light up a distant spot. Oh, and there's a strobe light and a couple of rolls of duct tape."

"Strobe light?" Michaels asks.

"Yeah, it's a navigation spare from one of the scouts. I replaced the capacitor a couple of days ago but haven't had the chance to run it down to the hangar. This fucker will near as blind you if you look directly at it."

Harris pulls the strobe out of a drawer and says, "It's set in a bell-shaped cowl to direct the flash away from the cockpit. Could be useful as a high-powered spotlight."

"Will it provide a continuous beam?" Hubbard asks.

"No, but it will light up an area the size of a football field for a split second. Damn thing goes off like a lightning strike. If these things are afraid of light, this strobe could be a lifesaver."

Lightning strike. Michaels finds his mind lingering on that point, but he's not sure why. There's something about the lightning on this planet that bugs him, some tiny thread unraveling, but before he can focus on that thought, Harris pulls out a battery the size of a shoebox, distracting him.

Harris connects two wires from the strobe to the terminals. One of the wires has a switch hanging from it. He hands the strobe, battery, and wires to Jacobs, saying, "Be careful which way you point this thing. The last thing we need is to be blinded for a couple of minutes."

Hubbard asks, "How long between flashes?"

"Ten, maybe twenty seconds on a battery like this. It takes some time for the capacitor to build up charge."

Vegas addresses Harris, saying, "Once you've fixed the junction box, find somewhere down there to hole up. No sense in risking a return journey. Just sit tight and wait for the cavalry."

"Roger that. We'll get this baby back online, and then she's all yours."

Harris pulls a strip of duct tape and speaks to Hubbard. "Come here. We'll tape down the penlights to keep our hands free."

Hubbard holds his arms away from his sides as Harris wraps tape around him, sticking on penlights. He sticks them on each shoulder, pointing one forward and the other backwards. Several penlights are strapped at points around his chest, shining down at his feet, illuminating a rough circle around him.

"You look like a Christmas tree," Michaels says.

"Or a high-tech hobo," Jacobs says.

"You're next," Harris says.

"The attacks we've seen have come from behind," Michaels says, and Harris positions a couple of the penlights so they face backwards.

"You guys are a modern day Tweedle-dee and Tweedle-dum," Vegas says with a grin on her face. "Sorry, I couldn't resist."

"That's really funny," Jacobs replies drily as Harris finishes taping penlights in place. Lights shine out at various angles, highlighting the ground around them, with more attention focused on the area behind them.

Vegas fits each of the men with a communications headpiece—a thin metal headset with a wireless camera mounted over the right ear. The built-in microphone will pick up a whisper.

There are only four penlights left when it comes time to set up Harris. Michaels tapes one to each shoulder, again facing forward and backwards, using plenty of duct-tape to hold them firmly in place.

As the three men prepare to open the door of the bridge, lights bounce around the command deck, reflecting off the displays. Hubbard and Harris have mining lasers slung over their shoulders, but Michaels doubts they'll get the chance to use them, or how effective they'll be, but if carrying them makes the two men feel safer, then so be it.

Harris lights the pilot light on his propane torch, and prepares to fire.

"Ready?" Michaels asks, standing by the door release.

"Ready as I'll ever be."

Hubbard stands behind Harris, holding the propane tank with both hands. In the increased gravity, it's difficult to carry anything far from one's center of gravity, and Hubbard has the tank in front of him, leaning against one leg. His arms are pulled taut, his shoulders hunched. The array of penlights with their beams flaring in different directions makes his appearance surreal. Jacobs stands behind Hubbard, but closer than Michaels expects. He's nervous. Although it's cool, sweat beads on his forehead. He peers past Hubbard and Harris, watching as the door opens slowly.

Harris isn't taking any chances. He isn't going to wait to be attacked. He unleashes a fireball from his propane torch, letting a short burst shoot through the narrow opening. The whoosh of the combustion and the smell of burning fuel add to the tension of the moment.

As the door opens, Harris edges forward, leading the way with the pilot light burning on the tip of his torch. Hubbard follows close behind him, trying to keep the fuel line slack between them. Jacobs looks back briefly as he follows them through the door. Michaels wonders if he'll see any of them alive again.

"I've got you on the monitor," Vegas says. "All three signals coming through clearly."

Harris stands immediately outside the bridge as the door closes behind them.

"Hubbard, eyes left. Jacobs, right," Harris says. Both men comply, giving Vegas a view of the T-junction in all directions.

"Nothing with enhanced vision," she says, flicking between camera modes.

"Good," is the reply, but Michaels isn't sure who spoke.

The three men proceed to walk down the central corridor rather than heading to the secondary access ways on either side of the craft. Harris fires a sharp burst and watches as a fireball spirals down the hallway, folding in on itself and billowing as it lights up the length of the walkway in fiery hues.

"Clear."

Slowly, they creep down the corridor. Their penlights are feeble against the darkness, barely pushing back the night around them. Michaels feels claustrophobic. Dark walls seem to close in around the men, boxing them in.

LITTLE GREEN MEN

"Something's wrong," Michaels says, watching the three men creep through the darkness.

Vegas switches off her microphone, raising an eyebrow as she says, "And you're just arriving at that conclusion now?"

"No, but I think we've missed something fundamental... I think I've missed the signs all around us."

"Signs of what?" Vegas asks, her eyes watching the three monitors intently.

Harris and Hubbard face forward. Jacobs is facing back toward the bridge. He holds the strobe light in one hand, the battery in the other, gripping them as though they're a life-support system.

"Lightning," Michaels muses, lost in thought, looking at the strobe light in Jacobs' trembling hand. There's something about the lightning on this planet that troubles him.

"Yeah, that's one hell of a storm out there," Vegas says. "According to the *Argo*, she's a persistent anticyclonic storm. Could have been raging for centuries, like Jupiter's Great Red Spot."

"Persistent," he repeats, feeling the pieces of the puzzle beginning to fall into place. "Constantly releasing vast amounts of electrical energy."

"I guess so," Vegas says, but she's more focused on the screens than on conversing with him. The look on her face is one of exhaustion. She rubs her eyes.

"What about the *Céleste*?" Michaels asks. "Doesn't that bother you?"

"Everything bothers me," Vegas replies. "I don't see where you're going with this."

"What if we're wrong? What if we've misunderstood everything that's happened here, and we're taking this the wrong way?"

"Taking what the wrong way?" Vegas asks.

"The *Céleste*. The little green men."

"Just what the hell are we dealing with?" Vegas asks, pulling herself away from the screens for a moment. Somehow, she's found her second wind. She locks eyes with him. He's always admired the steely determination in her leadership, and never more so than now. Most people would be intimidated by Vegas, afraid to speak up—not out of a fear of being wrong, but out of a fear of appearing stupid in front of her. Michaels has never thought that way. For him, being shown as wrong is an opportunity to be right. Her conviction is license for him to renew his thinking and reasoning. He's been wondering about the lightning. He'd initially noticed lightning striking the thermal pools with regular frequency. It was probably nothing, but reason demanded answers.

"It's the lightning that bothers me," he says.

"The lightning?"

"I think I may have overlooked something critical," he says.

"When you were out there in the thermal pools, you said there was life?" Vegas asks. "But not like this, right?"

"Yeah," Michaels replies. "Simple cellular life, maybe some kind of alien bacteria, but not this, nothing this highly developed. On Earth, biology took billions of years to go from single-celled creatures to multicellular life. Once we got to that point, though, life bloomed in every possible environment, but here there's just these little green men and some primordial sludge in a bunch of thermal pools."

"And that bothers you?" Vegas asks.

"Yes. I can't imagine these little green men are autotrophs—capable of sustaining life independent of a food chain. Given what we've seen of their physiology, that makes no sense. They have eyes, teeth. There should be an intricate food web, a matrix of predators and prey. Where's the ecology? Where are the supporting structures that allow for this level of biological sophistication?"

Vegas rolls her eyes. "Don't look at me," she says. "You're bothered by biology, I'm bothered by savage creatures sabotaging my ship! I'm bothered by the fact these alien carnivores are chewing on power cables and feeding on my crew."

"But don't you see that as an inconsistency?" Michaels protests. "How can they be carnivores? What is there for them to consume when we're not here?"

Vegas is silent.

"How can they have evolved for hundreds of millions of years to survive in a frozen wasteland, and yet have a taste for proteins that originated on a balmy Earth under entirely different chemical circumstances?"

"I don't know. You're the scientist. You tell me."

"The chemistry's all wrong. They'd need some kind of exotic antifreeze for blood. The cold, the intense pressure, the toxic cocktail in the atmosphere—these factors should have resulted in something entirely different from terrestrial life, something incompatible at a cellular level."

The radio crackles. Harris speaks in a whisper.

"We've reached medical."

"Can I?" Michaels asks, gesturing toward her headset.

Vegas hands him the microphone.

"Harris, how do I fire up the analytics control? Can I bring up 3D rendering on emergency power?"

"It'll chew through the reserves."

"This is important," Michaels says. "I think I'm on to something."

"Bring up a command prompt on the system console, look for

hive.start, *render.start* and *analytics.start*, and be sure to bring them online in that order. You'll have access to core historical records but none of the current sensor metrics. There's no way to get those until the main power comes back online."

"Got it," Michaels replies. "Oh, and Harris, don't engage these things. Whatever you do, don't attack them."

"Is there something you want to tell us?" Hubbard asks, jumping into the conversation, his voice quivering.

"Just following a hunch."

Michaels hands the headset back to Vegas who says, "Take it slow and easy out there."

"Roger that."

On the screen, Michaels and Vegas can see the flickering blue flame of the pilot light fighting off the darkness. The penlight beams light up isolated patches of the corridor, revealing the bloodstained floor and walls outside the medical center. The three men pass cautiously to one side of the darkened room. The sound of a metal tray being knocked over somewhere in the medical bay reminds them they're not alone.

"Whatever you're thinking," Harris whispers, knowing Michaels is listening in the background, "Think quick."

Michaels goes to work on the system console. It takes a few seconds for each of the programs to start so he watches the main monitor rather than watching the step-trace scrolling down the screen in plain text.

Harris creeps on, leaving Jacobs bringing up the rear.

Jacobs holds the inactive strobe light as if it were a gun. His hand is shaking. He fires the strobe, whether it's on purpose or by accident Michaels isn't sure, but a blinding flash illuminates the interior of the medical bay. Several of the creatures are staring back at him.

"Oh, fuck," he whispers under his breath. "Would have been better not to know."

On the screen, Michaels sees a hand strike Jacob across the chest. It's Hubbard, reprimanding him for firing the strobe.

Dark shapes move in the shadows.

"You're being followed," Vegas warns.

"Jacobs," Harris whispers. "Get your shit together."

Jacobs is silent.

On the bridge, the single, overhead light dims and flickers as the holographic projector starts up on the navigation desk.

"This had better be worth it," Vegas says, holding her hand over her microphone as she directs her comment at Michaels.

It has been years since Michaels has worked with a command line prompt in text mode. He's used to vocal commands and advanced-intent-interpretation. Having to be verbose and articulate precisely what he wants on a keyboard is cumbersome and error-prone.

Michaels searches through the folders on the computer until he finds the file holding the video and audio records of the attack on the ice. For now, he wants to forget about the *Céleste* and focus on what happened to Johnson. In the back of his mind, he feels as though he is working on a jigsaw puzzle with no picture on the box. Educated guesses are the best he can do, piecing together one section at a time. He starts a reconstruction routine, surprised he can remember the commands. The last time he did anything this archaic with a computer was back in college.

A partially reconstructed three-dimensional image appears before the two of them, floating above the nav desk. For those angles where there's no footage from either helmet camera, the image is transparent. Michaels watches the drama unfold from the vantage point of *The Eye of God*, a hypothetical spot about twenty feet above the astronauts. The computer reconstruction makes it look as though there had been a camera on a boom following them as they took the coral sample, waded through the thermal pool, out onto the frozen steppe, and into the full force of the storm, but just like a three-dimensional map, only those areas caught by their cameras show any real detail. Everything else is filled in based on complex algorithms that tend to oversimplify objects out of camera range.

Looking at the holograph, Michaels feels like one of the Greek gods sitting atop Mount Olympus, watching as lightning crackles above the image of the tiny astronauts staggering through the ice storm. It's hard to believe that was him barely eight hours ago.

He zooms in at the point the creatures begin their attack. As both men were facing forward, the majority of the reconstructed images lie in front of the astronauts struggling against the wind.

The computer depicts the incoming creatures as a blur,

providing clarity only to those surfaces that were exposed to the camera. The value of the reconstruction comes in understanding the speed and angle with which the aliens attacked, as well as their numbers. Michaels is fascinated to see the attack was coordinated. At the time it seemed random and haphazard, but the creatures came from both sides, swooping in one after the other, but always alternating sides.

Michaels watches in silence as Johnson's arm is severed in a flash of violence. One of the creatures leaps at the last minute—at least that's the way the computer renders the fragments of information caught by the cameras. The alien tears away his arm much like a dog would wrestle with a bone. Johnson drops to his knees and slumps onto the ice as his severed arm falls on a patch of exposed shale.

"I don't understand," Michaels mumbles. "His suit should have equalized with the pressure of the atmosphere around him. How did it seal?"

He remembers tending to Johnson inside the airlock on the scout. He'd seen frozen blood along with dark burns around the edge of the torn suit. He wants to understand what happened, but the holographic reconstruction is incomplete.

On the hologram, Johnson's helmet lies at an angle, half buried in the snow, half facing Michaels, allowing the video reconstruction to catch creatures racing past in the dark. Back then, it had taken Michaels a second to realize what had happened. A stream of creatures buffet him, tearing at his suit with their claws, scraping over his legs and boots before darting out, away from the spotlight on his helmet. Michaels is shocked. He thought it was the storm battering him and is horrified to realize how close he came to a suit puncture. The EVA suits could handle a small tear or a point-puncture, but seeing six-inch claws slashing at his legs, he shudders to see how close he came to dying.

He freezes the image.

"Can you enhance that?" Vegas asks with her microphone muted.

Michaels struggles to distance himself from what happened and view the scene objectively. Fear wells up inside him, but he breathes deeply, knowing he has to stay focused. Harris, Hubbard and Jacobs are depending on his advice.

"I'll increase gamma and brilliance," he says. "Let's get a good look at these little bastards."

Vegas glances at the monitors showing the progress of the team. Michaels can see she doesn't share his sense of dread. For her, the reconstruction is intriguing. To have lived through that moment, though, was harrowing. Watching himself come so close to dying leaves Michaels feeling empty. The contrast is not lost on him—his fear, her curiosity.

Michaels adjusts the scene, amplifying the light in the image. His fingers run over the keyboard, recalling commands he hasn't used in decades. He's numb, but he has to push on with the analysis. He has to give the rest of the crew a chance.

"We're at the fire suppression point," Harris whispers.

"Good," Vegas replies.

"Hubbard is grabbing some face masks. If we burn this place down, at least we'll get to enjoy front-row seats."

Michaels glances up, watching as dark shadows race back and forth across the T-junction in front of the team.

"Are you seeing that?" Harris asks. "Any recommendations?"

Vegas looks at Michaels.

"Single burst overhead."

"Michaels says avoid hitting any of the critters," Vegas replies, holding her finger on the transmit button built into the earpiece. "Try a burst overhead."

"Roger that."

Michaels holds his breath. He hopes he's right. At that moment, he's running on gut instinct, but he feels as though they need to keep the aliens at bay while avoiding a direct confrontation. Given the speed of these creatures, if they attack he has no doubt the three men would be overwhelmed. He only hopes these aliens have an innate sense of self-preservation. Certainly their aversion to light and the white clouds produced by the fire extinguisher suggest that.

Flames roar from the torch. Fire licks at the ceiling, curling along the walls, lighting the darkness with amber hues. Creatures snarl in the flickering light. There are dozens of them in the shadows. How many more lie out of sight is unknown.

"We are so *fucked*," Jacobs whispers.

"You optimist," Hubbard replies.

The overhead burst works, forcing the creatures back without harming them. Harris unleashes two more bursts, one back the way they came and another down the hallway leading to engineering. Acrid black smoke fills the air, drifting through the penlight beams. The three men continue cautiously forward, huddling together as though the light from their penlights provides warmth.

Michaels turns his attention back to the hologram. He reaches out with his hands, grabbing at the semi-translucent air and rotating his wrists. The computer responds, rotating the image accordingly.

"They're men!" Michaels says as the realization strikes his mind. He's seen these creatures before, but only ever in a flash, in a blur of motion, only ever out of the corner of his eye, or through adrenaline-soaked thinking. Now he sees them for what they are. "Johnson was right in his initial description. They're little green men, but that's impossible."

"Apparently not," Vegas replies, moving the microphone down away from her mouth to indicate she's addressing him and not the others.

Michaels shakes his head trying to grasp the implications of what he's seeing. For the first time, he has the opportunity to think rationally and clearly about these little green men. He finds his head spinning with possibilities, desperate to make sense of the images, desperate to reconcile the reconstruction he sees before him with his recollection of the attack on the ice and what he saw on the *Céleste*. Then there's the attack he witnessed outside the medical bay, and what Harris, Hubbard and Jacobs are risking as they creep through the bowels of the *Dei Gratia*. There's a pattern, a subtle thread just out of reach—teasing him. Tormenting him.

Michaels punches a few buttons and the scene moves on. He watches in awe at the holographic projection of himself planting a flare in the ice. A brilliant red light blazes out from that single point, casting long shadows on the frozen ground.

"Wait a minute," he says. "Johnson's arm is gone. Doesn't that strike you as strange?"

Vegas asks, "What part of any of this strikes you as normal?"

"No, no," Michaels replies, his mind alive with possibilities. "I mean, where is the arm? Doesn't it strike you as strange that his arm is gone? It was severed, we know that, but where is it? Where did it fall? It should be lying there in the snow beside him."

Vegas rubs her hands through her hair. She's exasperated.

"Is it really that important?" she asks.

"Everything's important," Michaels replies. "Everything we learn about these creatures shapes the way we interact with them. They took the arm as some kind of trophy, but why?"

The radio crackles. "We're running into more of these things," Harris says. "They're getting bolder. I don't know that the flames are going to keep them at bay."

Jacobs speaks, his voice stutters, spluttering. Michaels instinctively understands the fear he feels.

"Such a bad idea... Such a stupid idea to... to come out here in the dark."

Michaels looks at the view on Jacobs' monitor. Before the creatures stayed out of sight, now they move in the shadows.

"They're closing in," Hubbard says.

Harris fires another burst down the corridor. Patches of fire cling to the walls, smoldering as they burn out, and plunging the ship back into darkness.

"There has to be a reason for all this," Michaels says, reminding himself of Hubbard's earlier comment, and trying to steel his mind to look for answers. Fear clouds his thinking. He needs to think straight. He pulls himself away from the monitor and looks at the three-dimensional image of the little green men on the icy plain, trying to talk himself through the fear seizing his mind. "On—on Earth, life exploits reason. For the most part, it's the result of unconscious natural selection over countless generations, but there are reasons species succeed. Wherever we find life on Earth, it thrives for a reason. The reasons may be instinctive, opportunistic, or predatory, but there is *always* a reason behind an animal's actions, so the question is, why did they take Johnson's arm? They didn't kill him. They could have killed him, but they didn't. They wanted his arm."

Vegas gestures toward the hologram, spinning her hand as she speaks. "Can you roll it back? Zoom in and enlarge? See if you can bring in data from the other encounters to form a composite image of one of these things. Let's see what the hell we're dealing with."

Michaels punches his stubby fingers on the keyboard. A sense of purpose gives him hope. A little green man stands four feet tall above the navigation desk, frozen in place, slowly rotating in a counterclockwise direction.

"Look at their anatomy," Michaels says, immersing himself in the fascination of a scientific discovery. For a moment, his fear subsides. His hands no longer tremble. He could be sitting in a laboratory back at the university discussing a term paper. "Hubbard's right! Five fingers. Five toes."

Hubbard is an enigma. On the *Céleste,* Hubbard was so sure of himself, so confident. Back on the *Dei Gratia,* he's a different man—unsure, but willing to be brave. Hubbard didn't want to approach Medical, but he ran in to save Michaels, and he was the first to volunteer to join Harris.

Michaels mumbles, "Hubbard is the key to unraveling this."

"What?" Vegas asks, not catching his comment.

"Hubbard," he replies. "What the hell happened to him out there? How is he alive? Is he even human? Is he some alien impostor, or ghostly visitation?"

"He's no angel," Vegas says.

"Maybe if Hubbard is somehow still human, that would be the most remarkable outcome of all."

Vegas nods, watching the men inch their way toward engineering in the darkness.

The holograph of a little green man turns to face Michaels. Its teeth are bared, its sharp claws coiled, ready to lash out at him. Although he knows it isn't real, in that moment, Michaels feels as though the creature is watching him, as though intelligence looks through those dark, sullen eyes. A chill runs down his spine, and he distracts himself, losing his train of thought about Hubbard.

Michaels reaches in toward the figure and touches various points on the holographic image—the top of the shoulder, the elbow, the wrist, hand, and each of the fingers. As he does so, the computer automatically calculates lengths and relative ratios, displaying figures in the air beside the image. He mumbles to himself as Vegas says something to Harris. Michaels is so engrossed by the numbers floating before him he barely realizes she's speaking to the team. He touches the hip, the knee, and ankle, as well as measuring the length of the torso in relation to the rest of the body. He's curious about the diameter of the head, the ratio between the position of the nose, eyes, mouth, and ears.

"There are no visible genitals, but the proportions here are roughly human."

"What the *fuck* does that mean?" Vegas asks in a growl. "Are you saying these things are somehow related to us?"

Michaels shakes his head.

"No. But I am saying the proportions are what we'd find on a child of similar height. Look here, at the ratio between the forearm and the upper arm, it corresponds to the Golden Ratio, it's the same ratio we find in all life on Earth."

"What are the odds of that?" Vegas asks.

"It's not the ratio itself that's the problem," Michaels says thoughtfully, "it's the length the ratio is applied to. In this gravity, lengths shouldn't equal those on Earth. These creatures should be more stocky, better suited to load-bearing, not so thin and anemic."

"And yet there it is," Vegas replies, pointing at the holographic image.

Michaels finds his mind moving a million miles an hour, racing through a variety of possibilities. "This can't be right. If it is, we're talking about convergent evolution in different parts of the galaxy."

Vegas doesn't say anything. At a guess, she doesn't understand the concept.

"Convergent evolution has occurred a handful of times on Earth, but it's the exception rather than the norm. The norm is for animals that look similar to be related through a common ancestor. Humans and monkeys both have four fingers and a thumb because they share a common ancestor. They didn't develop four fingers and a thumb independently of each other as the chances of that occurring are next to nil. One would end up with six, the other two, or whatever.

"But there are some adaptations that are so crucial to survival they arise independently of each other. Dolphins and sharks both have superbly streamlined bodies even though these body shapes arose independently at vastly different times."

The fear is gone. Mentally, Michaels is on another planet.

"Eyes—sight is such an amazingly useful sense that it evolved at least twenty times, forming entirely different pedigrees. We, and all other mammals, have a blind spot inherited from a flaw introduced hundreds of millions of years ago, but the octopus doesn't. Its eye comes from a convergent pedigree. It developed separately, in parallel to ours, and never suffered from a blind spot."

"I don't see how this relates to our little green men," Vegas says.

"The point is, convergence on a common solution is possible, but this... this is impossible, this is not convergence, this is duplication. I mean, conceivably, there could be some forms of convergent evolution in different parts of the galaxy for common functions like sight, but even then, you'd expect them to center around different parts of the electromagnetic spectrum, depending on local conditions. But these creatures, they look like children. They're an exact physical copy. Look at him—he's got two eyes, two ears, a nose, and a mouth. Why not one eye, four ears and a mouth at the end of his hands? Why is he exactly like us?"

"A mouth at the end of your hand?" Vegas retorts. "Michaels, you're losing it."

"No, no. Butterflies taste with their feet," Michaels replies in rebuttal. "Think about all the incredible variety on Earth. Think about the radical differences between squid and crocodiles, or between bees and eagles. There are so many different lifeforms on Earth, it's astonishing. We should see even *more* variety between star systems, not less, but all we see is one, isolated life form that has roughly the same body plan as ours? I'm not buying it."

"Snap out of it!" Vegas growls. "Your crazy ideas aren't doing us any good. Whether you buy it or not, they're here, they're real, and they're killing people—murdering my crew!"

"But it's absurd to think this is real," Michaels counters. Vegas might be frustrated and angry, but Michaels can't ignore his scientific training. Everything he's observed screams of error. There are too many inconsistencies. There has to be another explanation. "Life on this planet is impossible."

"And yet it is possible," Vegas insists. "Here it is, right in front of us. We can see these creatures with our own eyes."

She pauses, rubbing her temples and breathing deeply. The stress is getting to both of them.

"Maybe there was some kind of celestial cross-pollination," she offers. "That's possible, right? Maybe millions of years ago, little green men visited Earth and we're somehow related to them."

"No, no, no." Michaels continues. "This isn't some low-budget science fiction film with actors running around in cheap plastic suits. You're not thinking clearly. Look at the climate. It reaches 320 below. No organic being of any kind can function in that environment."

"And yet they do," Vegas replies.

"And that's the problem," Michaels says. "They can't. It is not physically possible."

He thinks for a moment before continuing. "There is a scientific principle called deductive reasoning that says, *once you eliminate the impossible, whatever remains, no matter how improbable, must be true.*"

"Sherlock Holmes?" Vegas says with disbelief. "Seriously? You're drawing on fiction?"

"Although this phrase was made famous by Sherlock, it's more than fiction. It's the underlying principle behind numerous scientific theories, including relativity."

Vegas puts her hands on her hips. She's not convinced.

"Think about it. The speed of light is always the same regardless of motion. But that's impossible in classical physics. Speed is a measurement of the distance something travels divided by the time that trip took, right? Miles per hour. If you walk the length of a scout craft traveling at five hundred miles per hour, you're walking at two miles an hour within the craft, but at five hundred and two miles an hour for anyone watching you from the ground. And yet light shows no such variance."

"Is there a point to this?" she asks.

"Yes, yes. Light moves at exactly the same speed regardless of where or how you see it moving. That seems impossible until you consider something improbable, that either time or distance must change to allow light to remain at the same speed, and so we come to the bizarre, counterintuitive notion that time slows down in moving frames of reference. You see, if something looks impossible, it simply means there's an improbable explanation waiting to be uncovered."

"So if little green men are impossible," Vegas asks, "what improbable alternative is true?"

"That's what I'm trying to figure out," Michaels replies. "All I know is the evidence we have leads to one conclusion: *there are no little green men.*"

Harris speaks over the radio, saying, "Moving down to engineering."

"So what should I tell them?" Vegas asks, ignoring Harris and leaving her microphone muted. "You're saying none of this is real? Tell that to Johnson! Tell it to Summers! How can you say these things aren't real? You've seen these creatures firsthand—we all have."

Johnson. Summers. Michaels finds himself grasping at the loose threads of the problem, remembering the way they reacted to the little green men. He'd lumped Jacobs in along with them as those members of the crew most deeply affected by the presence of these alien creatures.

"Don't you see? That's the problem," he replies, slowly piecing the puzzle together. "We trust our eyes over science. But the existence of these little green men defies the laws of physics, chemistry, and biology—laws that have been universally proven time and again over the past five hundred years. It's as though we ran into Little Red Riding Hood on this frozen rock... If their existence is not scientifically possible then the only conclusion I can reach is that none of this is real."

"You're *fucking* insane," Vegas snaps, turning away from him and shaking her head as she walks toward the bulkhead. She paces for a few feet before swinging around and pointing at him as she yells. "I need answers. I've got men out there, risking their *goddamn* lives to bring this ship online, and they're trusting the advice we give them. What the *hell* do you want me to tell them? That this is all just a figment of their imagination?"

"I didn't say that," Michaels replies, feeling his blood boil. Anger surges through his veins. He bites his lip, struggling to articulate his thinking.

Vegas purses her lips. For a moment, he wonders if she's going to hit him. Light glistens in her eyes. The lines on her face are as hard as stone.

"What about the *Céleste*?" she demands. "How do you explain Hubbard dying and then being alive? What about what happened to you in the medical bay? Was that all just in your head?"

"Ah," Michaels says, pulling the conversation back a step, "What about the *Céleste*? Doesn't it strike you as strange that neither Hubbard nor Jacobs could make out the name of the ship, but Dr. Summers could? They were right there on the spot, and yet somehow they miss that critical detail. How could she make out the word *Céleste* over a crappy video link? How was that possible? I couldn't see it. Could you?"

"What are you saying?" Vegas demands. She must think he's crazy, and he half-wonders if the pressure has caused him to crack, but he feels as though he's on to something—on the cusp of unraveling the mystery. Consistency—since the birth of science, deductive reason has always been about consistent explanations of natural phenomena. That there's none in this situation drives him crazy, and he fights to piece together what's happened.

"What was the first thing Hubbard said when he walked onto the bridge?"

"I... ah, I don't know." Vegas replies.

"Precisely. We were so upset about seeing him die that his words were lost on us. He was concerned about Johnson being sedated, and yet if he'd been out on patrol he wouldn't have known about Johnson in the sickbay. For all he knew, we could have sent Johnson up to the *Argo* in a scout. Hubbard must have been in the medical bay before he walked onto the bridge. But that's impossible, right? How could he be in two places at once?"

Vegas speaks with ice cold determination. "We saw him die."

"Ah, yes. We did. Or did we?"

Michaels taps madly at his keyboard, searching for the flight logs from the hangar bay.

"And," he says. "Hubbard asked us, *'Why is Jacobs back out there alone?'* Hubbard wanted to know why Jacobs went back out on the ice a second time after you ordered the ships back here. Doesn't that strike you as strange?"

"This whole goddamn planet strikes me as strange," Vegas confesses.

Michaels finds the logs in the computer.

"Look," he says. "Here's the flight times. There's Hubbard and Jacobs leaving in Scout-2. There's my flight in Scout-3. Half an hour later, Scout-2 returns and refuels before going back out again."

He pulls up the video records from the hangar bay, jogging the footage so it matches the time of the refueling. There's only one figure visible in the cockpit of the scout.

"All this time, we've assumed Hubbard was lying, because we saw him go into the *Céleste* and die. Mentally, we've choked at reconciling the man we see before us now with that lonely death trapped between floors, but we were wrong."

Vegas looks lost. Her eyes are blank—staring ahead, but not registering her surroundings.

"So what the hell is happening?" she asks in a daze.

"First Contact," Michaels replies, his voice stiffening with confidence. "We're in the midst of making first contact with an extraterrestrial intelligence that is vastly beyond anything we've ever imagined, and that's the problem. Our fears imagine the worst, and the worst becomes reality."

"I... I don't understand," Vegas says.

"Think about First Contact between radically different societies on Earth. They all start with confusion and conflict."

Vegas disagrees. "Columbus didn't run into hostile natives."

"Columbus *was* the hostile native from Spain!" Michaels counters, "It's all a matter of perspective. Columbus took slaves, plundered gold, and murdered those Indians that wouldn't trade with him."

Vegas is silent. Michaels goes on, thinking out loud.

"First Contact exposes motives on both sides of the divide, motives that reach beyond the moment. It was Hubbard that first alerted me to the possibility that we're dealing with something more than a mere skirmish with indigenous life forms. He was reading about Captain James Cook discovering *Terra Nullius*, the great empty southland of Australia—only the land wasn't empty. When Cook tried to go ashore he was met with violent opposition. Peaceful communication took time. It took several weeks before Cook could converse with the aborigines and build a common understanding of the most basic items: fish, spears, men, women, children."

"And you think that's what's happening here?" Vegas asks.

"Yes. Fear is contagious. Think about it. These creatures had no way to get onboard our ship, and yet here they are. They didn't come in through an airlock, they haven't breached the hull, so how the *hell* did they get inside?

"And their physiology is all wrong. If their natural environment is negative three hundred degrees, how can they operate comfortably in our balmy eighty degrees? We know of no life form on Earth that can survive such extremes, and with good reason, because cellular chemistry changes radically under such thermal variations, especially with such radically different atmospheric pressures. These creatures have never had a highly oxygenated environment like ours, and yet they can survive in our atmosphere with no side effects. I don't buy it. That's just not possible. They should be suffering from something like the bends, or altitude sickness, or poisoning, or something, but they shouldn't be able to switch between the two environments so easily. We need a spacesuit to go out there. They should need something similar to come in here."

"So they're a figment of our imagination?" Vegas asks.

"Not our imagination," Michaels replies. "Our deepest fears. When we were on the ice, Johnson joked about little green men, but it was no joke. He was terrified something was going to jump out at him."

"You're saying they attacked him because he was afraid?" Vegas asks, clearly surprised by the concept.

Michaels pauses, thinking about her question. He's improvising, articulating his thoughts on the fly and surprising himself as a coherent concept distills from the chaos. "Not exactly," he replies, walking through the logic. "Johnson cut a coral limb. They responded in kind, cutting off his arm."

"So they perceived his action as a threat—an attack?"

"I guess so."

"And Jacobs?" Vegas asks. "How does he fit into your little hypothesis?"

"Jacobs was afraid of going inside that abandoned freighter. He needed someone else to explore the *Céleste,* someone brave enough, and that someone was Hubbard. Our Hubbard never set foot inside that ship. Jacobs was desperately afraid of what he'd find—he needed a proxy. He needed someone else to go onboard so Hubbard appeared beside him."

"I don't get it," Vegas says. "Why was there an empty star freighter there in the first place? Where did it come from?"

"From Dr. Summers," Michaels replies. "She was desperately afraid we'd find something out there on the ice, so we did. She's the one that made the connection between the *Dei Gratia* and the *Céleste.* That had to be something eating away at the back of her mind. She knew the stories of a ghost ship on Earth—the *Mary Céleste*—and she projected those fears onto us.

"Whatever this thing is, it feeds off our fears, but this is more than a group hallucination—it's a group construct. Our fears have taken on a life of their own."

"I don't know," Vegas says. "I'm not convinced. I mean, if you're right then all this is a fabrication—a self-induced nightmare."

"What class of ship was the *Céleste*?" Michaels asks.

"C-Class."

"Really?" Michaels replies, tapping on the keyboard. "That's not what Harris said when he pulled up her records. He said she was a frigate, remember? A military vessel. But no one listened to him. We believed our eyes, not our ears. We should have questioned him further instead of assuming he was wrong."

Michaels brings up an image of the *Céleste* from the computer archive. The three-dimensional image before them morphs into a warship, bristling with armament to protect itself from close-quarter pirate attacks.

"We saw what we wanted to see," Vegas mumbles.

"Yes. We saw what our weakest minds feared," Michaels replies. "Jacobs did his apprenticeship on a C-Class freighter, he knew the layout, so that's what he wanted to see—and that's what we all saw."

Vegas says, "So these things... these creatures... they're not the alien we're dealing with?"

"Ah," Michaels replies, liking her thinking. "Now we're getting somewhere."

"Jesus," she says as the realization hits.

Vegas switches on her microphone, positioning it barely an inch from her lips. She speaks with slow deliberation.

"Harris. Listen carefully," she says. "These things are feeding off our fears. Nothing is what it seems. You need to–"

Jacobs cuts her off, yelling, "Look out!"

Several of the creatures lunge at them. Claws cut through the air as the aliens roar, baring their teeth.

Harris waves his makeshift flamethrower at them, releasing a burst of fire in an arc over their heads and causing them to scatter. Beyond the flames, little green men snarl. Black smoke billows through the air.

"Pull back," Harris cries over the top of Vegas trying desperately to reason with him. There's yelling. In the darkness, numerous items are knocked over, crashing to the floor.

Hubbard yells, "In here." He retreats blindly into a darkened doorway, dragging the gas cylinder along the grating on the floor. Jacobs squeezes through the doorframe behind him, pushing Harris to one side in his panic. Vegas is still trying to get their attention, but the three men are talking at once.

"Harris. Harris, listen to me."

"Over there," Jacobs points, and Harris fires a burst to cover their retreat. Once he's inside, Hubbard slams the door, but not before Harris lets a final fireball loose from the torch, sending flames shooting through the air. Fire lashes at the far wall as the creatures scramble away.

"Are we safe?" Jacobs asks.

Hubbard spins around, his feeble flashlight rippling across desks and chairs, shelving, and darkened video consoles.

"I think so. I hope so."

Outside, they can hear the creatures pounding against the door, scratching at the handle. Harris flicks the lock, sealing them in the room.

"Where are you?" Vegas asks, looking at a schematic diagram of the *Dei Gratia* on the one working computer.

"Uh," Harris replies, turning and looking around him. "It's the control room for engineering."

"Listen," Vegas says. She's trying to explain what she and Michaels have learned, wanting to compress the concept into as few words as possible, but she keeps getting cut off.

"They're under the floor," Jacobs cries, his camera pointing down at the grating. Dark green claws grip the steel grates, tugging at them, trying to dislodge them.

"Listen to me," Vegas orders over the microphone, but no one does. Shelving falls to the grating, sending out a deafening clatter.

Michaels is frustrated, he wants to grab the microphone from her and yell at them. He feels as if the exertion of brute force here will have an impact there, but it won't. His efforts are futile, but the urge borders on overwhelming. He jumps to his feet, clutching at the air before Vegas, gesturing for her to surrender the microphone. She holds out her hand, appealing for patience. She has this under control, or so she thinks. He isn't so sure, and yet what can he do? Just like the fears of the crew, Michaels finds himself reacting with primitive, primal impulses. It is as though he can bend reality to his will. The realization that he can't is crippling, and he gnashes his teeth in anguish.

"You need to–" Vegas begins, but again she's cut off.

Hubbard yells, "We're trapped! There's no way out." Vapor forms from his breath, highlighting how cold the craft is becoming. Jacobs is shivering, but whether from fear or the cold, Michaels can't tell.

"Pilot light's dead," Harris says. "The nozzle's blocked."

Harris hangs the torch on his belt and pulls the mining laser from his shoulder. He tries to power it up. A tiny blue LED light flickers, but fades quickly to red, and then disappears. "What the hell?" He smacks the side of the laser on a bench top, willing it to life, but the batteries have failed in the rapidly plummeting temperature.

On the monitor, Michaels can see Hubbard peering through a window overlooking the two floors that make up the engineering bay. The penlights on his shoulder illuminate dozens of vicious faces on the other side of the window. Dark green fists pound on the Plexiglas.

Jacobs backs into the corner. Mentally, he's overwhelmed—laughing, cackling—losing his mind to the rush of fear.

"It's Jacobs," Vegas yells pointing at the screen as though they can see her gesture. "Johnson and Summers are gone. He's the only one left. He's attracting them."

"What?" Harris cries, yelling over the din in the small room. He holds his finger over his ear, trying to hear her properly. "What the hell are you talking about?"

Hubbard turns to look at Jacobs, as does Harris. Their penlights illuminate him for the cameras. Sweat beads on Jacobs' brow in spite of the cold. His face is pale. His eyes are bloodshot. Michaels has seen that look before. It's the same, crazy, deluded grin Johnson had in the medical bay.

"I don't understand," Harris calls over the sound of the creatures fighting to get into the control room.

"It was never Hubbard," Vegas replies. "Hubbard never set foot on that ghost ship. Michaels retrieved the flight logs. It was Jacobs. Jacobs went out there alone."

"You're crazy," Jacobs wails, pointing at them. "All of you. You're crazy. Of course Hubbard was there, you saw him."

Hubbard steps up to Jacobs, taking a good look at him. Jacobs is shaking. His eyes are wide with fear.

"This is insane," Jacobs says over the coms link. "You're blaming me for all this? Surely, you don't believe Michaels. It's Michaels fault. He should have never gone in that thermal pool."

Hubbard ignores the creatures clamoring to get into the room, eyeing Jacobs with suspicion.

"Michaels has been wrong about everything," Jacobs protests. "We should have been fighting these aliens from the very start. We should arm the mining lasers for short bursts and take these bastards on. Yeah, that's it. If we're going to go down, we go down fighting."

"Shut up, Jacobs," Harris snaps.

"Yeah," Hubbard says, his voice unusually calm. For him, everything seems to make sense.

"What are you telling me?" Harris asks, turning away from Jacobs and directing his comment at Vegas and Michaels.

Michaels can't help himself, he starts talking to Vegas as though he's talking to the whole team, even though none of them can hear him.

"Don't you see," he says, "It was pride that got us into this. We thought we could come down here and strip mine the planet for its volatiles. It didn't matter what we had to do to get them, we could just do it regardless. For billions of years, this planet has been untouched—and we come along and want to suck it dry in a few days."

"Don't go all eco on me," Vegas retorts. "It's a *goddamn* rock!"

"But it's not a lifeless rock. And pride, that's what started all this. Johnson was swept up in it—so was I. Don't you see? There are no monsters on this planet. We're the monsters."

"What's he saying about monsters?" Harris asks, having backed up into the corner of the room beside Hubbard. Jacobs has his hands up, fiddling with his beard. His actions are manic—shaky and erratic.

"Monsters," he mumbles, his face twitching. "They're monsters. We need to kill them."

Harris and Hubbard ignore the sound of the aliens clawing at the windows and the door, focusing intently on Jacobs. Both men can see it—the fear in his eyes.

"It's about us," Michaels yells. "We thought all this was about the little green men, but it's not—it's about us. Think about it. Why did they chop off Johnson's arm?"

Vegas is silent. She pulls the microphone from her head, holding it by her side. A dim yellow light on the side of the microphone indicates it's in standby mode. Michaels isn't sure when she switched off her microphone, but the green light beside the speaker in the ceiling indicates the omnidirectional microphones on the bridge are broadcasting his words. He answers his own question, saying, "Because we chopped off a coral limb."

"You're saying they're copying us?" Harris asks over the radio.

"Not copying—responding, reacting, communicating."

"He's wrong," Jacobs says, spluttering and spitting as he speaks. "They tried to kill Johnson. They murdered that—that nurse in the sickbay, and now they're coming for us."

"They're feeding off our strongest emotions," Michaels explains. "There are no little green men—only our fears."

Jacobs screams, "They're inside!"

Hubbard and Harris turn. Dozens of little green men creep forward, cornering the three men behind a stainless steel workbench. With teeth bared and clawed hands out in front of them, they step forward like lions stalking prey. Hubbard and Harris push themselves back against the wall next to Jacobs, trying to shelter behind the bench.

Michaels flinches, yelling. "Look at what's happening. Look at reality. The window's intact. The door's closed. There's no loose grating."

"How the *fuck* did they get in?" Jacobs moans.

"You brought them in," Michaels tells him, still yelling on the bridge. "Jacobs, listen to me: there are no little green men. What we're seeing here is the initial attempt of an advanced alien species trying to communicate with us in terms we understand. We thought of little green men—they obliged and gave us little green men. These are our fears, our nightmares, our horrors brought to life."

Harris struggles with the pilot light on the propane torch. Flames flicker as gas begins to flow, and he sends a burst across in front of the aliens, keeping them at bay. Dark eyes peer back at them. The flame dies. Harris strikes the nozzle on the countertop, trying to clear soot from the outlet.

"You're saying, all this is fabricated?" Hubbard asks.

"We caused this?" Harris cries into his microphone.

"They're created from our most passionate, instinctive, emotional responses," Michaels says, watching as the creatures inch closer, their sharp claws outstretched, slowly breaking into the feeble beams given off by the penlights. "They're shaped by our collective response. They're the culmination of our darkest thoughts—the personification of our fears."

"So we're fueling all this?" Harris asks, his outstretched hand trembling as one of the creatures touches at his fingers.

"Yes," Michaels responds, seeing Harris fighting his fear. "What you're seeing is real, but it's not reality. You've got to believe me. You're seeing our group construct, that's the only logical possibility consistent with the laws of science."

The alien examines his fingers with the same interest Harris shows, moving in almost a mirror image, but snarling like a tiger. Harris keeps his trembling hand out in a feeble attempt to keep the vicious, but curious creature at bay. He crouches, dropping to the same height as the aliens, and they skitter back a few feet in response to his motion. They're skittish, eyeing him warily, as wild animals once feared man, unsure how *Homo sapiens*, so weak and vulnerable, could ever dominate the food chain.

"You're saying they're real," Harris says, "but they're not part of reality."

"Yes," Vegas replies, speaking before Michaels can. "It's the planet. It's alive!"

"She's right," he calls out, yelling as though he's shouting down the hallway rather than speaking over the radio. Vegas has figured it out. This is the final piece of the puzzle. The planet itself is the unseen puppet master behind the appearance of the little green men. It's the intelligence that crafted the *Céleste* from the mind of Dr. Summers and Jacobs.

Jacobs laughs like a maniac.

"You believe that?" he says. "Hah! You're mad. You're as crazy as Michaels."

Neither Harris nor Hubbard laugh, but a couple of the creatures do, mimicking Jacobs.

Hubbard whispers, "We've done this to ourselves!"

Jacobs' laugh grows from a giggle to a chuckle. He snorts. The aliens mirror his response, although they seem to cackle with wicked intent. Rather than finding Jacobs funny, they seem to relish the release of emotion.

"They're feeding off him," Hubbard says to Harris.

Snarling, the little green men creep closer. Jacobs continues his deranged laughter. Spittle drips from his beard.

"Summers and Johnson are gone," Michaels says, reiterating the point Vegas made. "There's only Jacobs left."

"We can't stop them," Harris says, looking at Hubbard.

The little green men lunge at the astronauts, racing forward to kill them, but Hubbard ignores the attack. Instead of lashing out at the aliens, he pushes Jacobs against the wall, and slams the butt of his mining laser into the side of Jacobs' head. The blow is brutal. Bones crack. Jacobs slumps to the floor with his eyes rolling into the back of his head. He rocks on his side, collapsing on the grating, with blood oozing from the base of his skull.

Harris faces the aliens. Hubbard swings the mining laser around, but the creatures take on a ghost-like appearance. They shimmer and fade from sight, laughing as they disappear into the darkness.

EPILOGUE

Michaels stands on the bridge of the *Argo* as it swings around the night side of the planet, orbiting well over four thousand miles above the surface. Lightning crackles in the clouds below him, rippling through the dark. Flashes of light reveal billowing cloud banks swirling in the turbulent atmosphere.

Vegas walks up beside him, saying, "Penny for your thoughts?"

"Oh, yeah."

"Philips has given the green light for your plan to use satellites in various orbits to communicate with the planet by interacting with its magnetic field."

Michaels nods, still lost in thought.

Vegas asks, "Do you really think this will work?"

"I don't know, but imaging has shown the network of flooded brine caves and fractured caverns have an uncanny resemblance to the complexity of our own neurons. Lightning seems to drive the system like a heartbeat, constantly firing the synapses."

"Lightning can do that?" Vegas asks.

"Yes. Our own minds are warm, wet circuits, flickering with electrical pulses, so yeah, I think so. On Earth, there are over eight million lightning strikes a day! That's over a hundred hits every second, but the planet is so big, they seem infrequent to us. Here, I'm detecting in excess of a billion discharges every twenty-seven hours. There's so much electrical activity from the storms circling the planet, I suspect the planet's own electromagnetic field is going to be our best way to talk to it. If we can get its attention and establish a baseline for communication, we'll have the chance to talk to an intelligence unlike anything we've ever imagined."

Vegas asks, "What would have happened if we had used those mining lasers down there?"

"We wouldn't have killed them," Michaels says flatly. "You can't kill something that's not alive. The little green men would have reacted adversely to being attacked and would have torn us apart."

Vegas nods. "So we were like a flea on a dog's back?"

"More like bacteria in someone's bloodstream," Michaels answers. "I suspect the little green men were the planet's immune response kicking into action."

"And you really think it's alive?" Vegas asks. "The entire planet? That seems bizarre."

"From our perspective, it is bizarre," he replies. "But what is life? These bodies of ours are spacesuits, housing a conscious being in an intricate life support system made from flesh and bone. We're composite creatures, built from trillions of individual cells to form a cohesive whole. We're just as extraordinary—just as unlikely."

"What do you think it makes of us?" Vegas asks.

"I don't know. I doubt it even knew we were down there, in the same way our bodies combat dozens of microbial attacks every day without us realizing."

"And now?"

"I think it knows we're here in orbit. It'll understand we're not just another moon, or a captured asteroid. It'll have seen us moving under our own steam, and will know there's an intelligence here. I suspect it's looking forward to chatting as much as we are."

"Well," Vegas says. "We've got plenty of time to test your theory. Philips is overruling the exploration portion of the mission and keeping us here in orbit, feeding everything back to the Hub. So much for settling new worlds. Looks like we'll be staying here for at least a decade until relief arrives."

"Given what we've seen so far," Michaels replies with a smile, "I think there's going to be plenty for us to do. I don't think the planet is going to disappoint."

Harris and Hubbard walk past. Harris has his arm over Hubbard's shoulder. They're sweating, carrying squash racquets. They must have just finished a game in the zero-g chamber. Jacobs is with them, joking about the game. They acknowledge Michaels and Vegas as they walk on toward the dormitory.

"How's Johnson?" Michaels asks Vegas.

"Summers says he's doing well," she replies. "They're fitting him with a cybernetic arm tomorrow, but I don't think you'll see him volunteering for surface missions again."

"Me neither," Michaels laughs.

He turns away from the dome, leaving the turbulent planet behind him. Out of the corner of his eye, he spots flashes of lightning. Strands of electricity ripple across the top of the cloud banks thousands of miles beneath the *Argo*. For a moment, Michaels could swear he heard someone else laughing as well.

THE BEGINNING

AFTERWORD

Firstly, my thanks to those beta-readers who took the time to provide invaluable insights into this novella. In no particular order, they are: Brian Wells, Bruce Simmons, One Pagan, TJ Hapney, Jamie Canubi, John Walker, Tibor Koch, Jae Lee, Deborah Ann Longe, Terry Grindstaff and Damien Mason. The cover art is by Jason Gurley. My thanks also go to my editor Ellen Campbell, who first reached out to introduce herself to me after spotting a couple of typos in this book, and then went on to edit the story several times over, polishing and refining its content.

Brian Wells, Tibor Koch and John Walker also provided technical input, assisting with the accuracy of the scientific concepts discussed in this novel. That said, all errors are unquestionably mine.

I hope you've enjoyed this novella as much as I have. I thought you might like to learn a little about how this story came into being. The pop-culture references and profanity are a ruse—a feint. Everything about this story is intended to lull the reader into a sense of complacency so they don't see the twist coming at the end. It's *Aliens*, it's *Event Horizon*, it's *The Thing*, when in reality, nothing is what it seems and there are no Little Green Men.

Little Green Men has an unusual pedigree as far as stories go, one that reaches back thousands of years. Plato originally proposed that people could be understood as tripartite beings, comprised of logic, the spirit/soul, and animalistic instincts such as hunger, thirst, love and anger. Plato saw these primary characteristics as being in conflict for dominion over the individual. Shakespeare took this concept further in *The Tempest*, examining the lives of Prospero (representing the rule of logic), Ariel (the sensitive spiritual side of life), and Caliban (the carnal monster). Vegas, Harris and Michaels are Prospero, Dr. Summers and Hubbard are Ariel, while Jacobs along with the Little Green Men and the planet itself are Caliban—the monster unleashed.

Sigmund Freud latched onto these distinctions as well, speaking of these three aspects of human nature as the id, ego, and superego. Then in 1956, Cyril Hume wrote the screenplay for *The Forbidden Planet*, which explored the "monster of the id," echoing Shakespeare's *The Tempest*. Michael Crichton also explored this concept in *Sphere*, looking at how First Contact could be tainted by our own innate fears and desires. I've extended this same idea further in *Little Green Men*, exploring how our own fears may blur our recognition of alien life.

Writers find inspiration in a lot of different areas. For me, writers like Alistair Reynolds provide breadth of vision, while others like Hugh Howey have a depth of characterization I admire. There are three standout writers, though, that have shaped my novels: Carl Sagan, Michael Crichton, and Philip K. Dick. And I've written several novels specifically in homage to them. Anomaly for Carl Sagan,

Feedback for Michael Crichton, and Little Green Men for Philip K. Dick.

Philip K. Dick (1928-1982) is an American science fiction writer, best known for the Hollywood adaptations of his stories in *Bladerunner (Do Androids Dream of Electric Sheep?), Total Recall (We Can Remember It for You Wholesale), Minority Report, Paycheck, A Scanner Darkly, Next,* and *The Adjustment Bureau.* His influence on the science fiction genre has been profound, with films like *Terminator* being loosely based on his *Second Variety.* Even such British classics as *Red Dwarf* owe a debt to the works of Philip K. Dick, with stories such as *A Maze of Death* and *The Colony* being forerunners of *Better Than Life* and *Polymorph.*

Philip struggled with drug addiction and mental illness, and died tragically from a stroke at the age of 53. I love his quirky short stories, and wrote *Little Green Men* as a tribute to his career in science fiction. For me, Philip K. Dick's stories are the essence of classic scifi. In particular, his *Twilight*-esque stories *Beyond Lies the Wub, Mr. Spaceship, The Skull* and The Colony inspired me to write science fiction.

If you're interested in reading some of Philip's works, you can find them available as free ebooks on Gutenberg.

Please take the time to leave a review of Little Green Men on Amazon. Your opinion is important. Your thoughts and impressions of this book will influence other readers far more than anything I say. As an independent author, I have limited means of reaching new readers. If books like this are going to become popular, it's because of you the reader, getting behind them. If you've enjoyed this story, make your voice heard by leaving a review, and tell a friend to grab a copy.

Thank you for supporting independent science fiction.

Printed in Great Britain
by Amazon